Praise for Christopher Stasheff

A Wizard in the Way

"The latest in Stasheff's popular 'Wizard' series provides a fast-paced plot, likable protagonists, and the expected blend of medieval fantasy and space opera."   —*Library Journal*

"Another entertaining combination of science fiction and fantasy in a universe where the mundane, magical, and technological live side by side. Anyone who relishes an action adventure tale set on a distant planet in a far away galaxy will want to read this book and it's predecessors."
     —*Midwest Book Review*

A Wizard in Midgard

"A witty tale of medieval space colonies and political intrigue. . . . If this is your first encounter with the rogue wizard, it will not be your last!"   —*Realms of Fantasy*

"A fast-paced action tale."   —*Absolute Magnitude*

A Wizard in Mind

"Stasheff has a knack for crafting a lighthearted, action-filled tale."   —*Library Journal*

"Stasheff's pacing is brisk, his historical literacy high, and his wit abundant and dry as ever. . . . Bodes well for further Magnus Gallowglass adventures."   —*Booklist*

BOOKS BY CHRISTOPHER STASHEFF

THE WARLOCK

*The Warlock in Spite
of Himself
King Kobald Revived
The Warlock Unlocked
Escape Velocity
The Warlock Enraged
The Warlock Wandering
The Warlock Is Missing
The Warlock Heretical
The Warlock's Companion
The Warlock Insane
The Warlock Rock
Warlock and Son*

THE ROGUE WIZARD

*A Wizard in Mind
A Wizard in Bedlam
A Wizard in War
A Wizard in Peace
A Wizard in Chaos
A Wizard in Midgard
A Wizard and a Warlock
A Wizard in the Way
A Wizard in a Feud*

THE WARLOCK'S HEIRS

*A Wizard in Absentia
M'Lady Witch
Quicksilver's Knight
The Spell-Bound Scholar*

STARSHIP TROUPERS

*A Company of Stars
We Open on Venus
A Slight Detour*

THE RHYMING WIZARD

*Her Majesty's Wizard
The Oathbound Wizard
The Witch Doctor
The Secular Wizard
My Son the Wizard
The Haunted Wizard
The Crusading Wizard
The Feline Wizard*

THE STARSTONE

*The Shaman
The Sage*

CHRISTOPHER STASHEFF

A WIZARD IN A FEUD

A TOM DOHERTY ASSOCIATES BOOK
NEW YORK

This is a work of fiction. All the characters and events portrayed in this book are either products of the author's imagination or are used fictitiously.

A WIZARD IN A FEUD

Edited by Jenna A. Felice

A Tor Book
Published by Tom Doherty Associates, LLC
175 Fifth Avenue
New York, NY 10010

www.tor.com

Tor® is a registered trademark of Tom Doherty Associates, LLC.

ISBN: 0-812-54152-9

First edition: July 2001
First mass market edition: February 2002

Printed in the United States of America

0 9 8 7 6 5 4 3 2 1

A Wizard

in a Feud

1

M"agnus, we have an emergency."

Magnus d'Armand looked up at the source of the calm voice. There was nothing there, of course—only a woodland scene in a gilded frame; the loudspeakers were hidden. "What sort of emergency, Herkimer?"

Across the expanse of thick, dark red carpet, Alea looked up from the scrolling print in front of her padded velvet armchair. She wore lounging pajamas of silk that only emphasized her height; there was no need to minimize it when her companion was nearly seven feet tall himself. She had a long, bony face framed in long, lustrous dark hair.

Magnus glanced at her, then glanced away to hide the admiration in his eyes—he was still unsure as to the nature of the heartbreak that had made her so wary of men and he was determined not to alarm her. She did seem to be past the worst of it, though there were still moments of hostility in her manner, and she still seemed too quick to argue minor points. But he was determined to prove himself a good friend and reliable companion—and safe. He mustn't let her see how much he was aware of the generous curves in that long figure or how exquisite he thought the bone structure of her face.

Besides, he had memories of his own, reasons to avoid intimacy.

Fortunately, the ship's computer distracted him with its answer. "There is a malfunction in my central processing unit, Magnus."

Magnus stiffened and saw the look of alarm on Alea's face. Amazing that a woman of a medieval society had learned so much of modern technology in two short years! "How serious is the malfunction, Herkimer?"

"There is no way to tell, Magnus. It has resisted my standard diagnostic programs. It will require extended analysis."

"We'd better plan for the worst," Alea said. "Any breakdown in the computer could threaten the life-support systems."

"Yes, and at any moment." Magnus frowned. "What functions are impaired, Herkimer?"

"Only memory so far, Magnus. I attempted to retrieve records of our last expedition but could not even bring up the name of the planet."

"It was Oldeira, and we limited the power of magician-despots by introducing Taoism," Alea told him.

"Datum entered," Herkimer acknowledged, then immediately said, "I could not even bring up the name of the planet."

Magnus's and Alea's gazes met with alarm. "The memory-sector is so corrupted that it can't even hold new data!" she exclaimed.

"And if Herkimer can't diagnose it, there's no way to tell whether or not it will spread to other functions," Magnus said. "If he forgets the rate at which he's supposed to be feeding us air or gets the nitrogen-oxygen proportions wrong, we could wind up having a very sound sleep indeed."

"We have to land!"

"Let's hope we can." Magnus raised his voice again. "Can you initiate a scan for livable planets, Herkimer?"

"Scanning," the computer responded. A few seconds later, it said, "There is a G-4 star less than a light-year distant."

"That's the same stellar type as Terra's sun," Alea said. "Does it have any planets, Herkimer?"

"Three," the computer answered, "with an asteroid belt between the second and the third, which is a gas giant."

"Tidal forces tore a fourth planet apart." Magnus nodded.

"Or prevented it from ever forming," Alea countered. "How about the other two, Herkimer? Is either of them hospitable to Terran-based life?"

"One is very compatible," the computer answered. "In fact, it is so close a match to Terra that I deduce it has been terra-formed."

"Lost Colony!" Alea cried.

"There is no record of a Terran colony at this location," Herkimer acknowledged.

"Land on that planet," Magnus told him. "It will keep us alive if anything goes wrong."

"Shore leave!" Alea's eyes lit. "Four months aboard ship is too long."

Magnus caught his breath; she seemed to glow in her eagerness, more vibrant, more alive than any woman he had known. He wondered why he found her so much more beautiful now than when he had first met her hiding in the forests of Midgard. He decided that it must be the effects of good nutrition and decent living conditions. He wrenched his mind back to the problem at hand and said, "There may be people there, too. Time for me to become Gar Pike again."

"Surely you don't think there will be anybody looking for Magnus d'Armand on a retrograde colony that's not even on the charts!"

"You can never tell where SCENT may have an agent," Magnus answered. "There are disadvantages to having a price on your head, especially when the organization who's offering that price counts you as a turncoat and rogue."

"Disadvantages?" Alea asked sourly. "What advantage could there be, to being a wanted man?"

"That depends on who is doing the wanting." Magnus met

her gaze for an instant before he turned away. "Let's go check our packs."

Herkimer's landing orbit took him over the daylit side of the planet three times—more than enough for him to spy on the locals with his electron telescope, and to fabricate copies of what he saw there. So, by the time he hovered over the middle of the dark side and landed the great golden disk that was their space-ship, Gar and Alea were decked out in broad-brimmed hats, loose shirts and trousers, and Black Watch plaid jackets.

"I just hope none of the locals wear this pattern," Alea said as they went down the gangway.

"If they do, we'll see if we can buy some other ones." Gar felt the gold nuggets in his pocket, currency on virtually any world. He hiked his pack a little higher on his shoulders and looked down at the unwieldy form of the flintlock rifle cradled in his arm. "Herkimer, are you sure this is how these people carry their weapons? I should think they'd be in danger of blowing away their own feet!"

"It is customary not to cock the hammer until you intend to fire, Magnus," the computer's voice said from behind them.

"We'll have to put in some target practice as soon as there's light," Alea said nervously. "This has to be the most clumsy weapon I've ever handled!"

"It must be effective," Magnus sighed. He frowned around at the forest bordering their clearing. There was no moon, but the sky blazed with five times as many stars as Terra's, and by their light he was able to make out a trail straggling across the meadow and into the wood. "Let's go there." He pointed. "We don't want people to find us in a meadow where the grass has been crushed flat by a spaceship's downdraft."

"And keep our eyes open for renegade locals?" Alea asked.

"Someone on the run always makes a good guide," Gar agreed. "That is, provided he's not on the run for being a gen-uine criminal."

"Well, I do have to say that much for a planet where everybody is trying to kill everybody else," Alea said. "They're not likely to have slaves who are trying to escape."

"No, but there might be someone who's been cut off from his own side." Gar resettled his rifle, grimaced at its awkwardness, and said, "Let's go."

They started off into the night, Alea with a thrumming eagerness inside; she still had not tired of seeing strange places and new peoples.

"Magnus," Herkimer's voice said behind them.

They turned to look, surprised.

"What is it, Herkimer?" Gar asked.

"I have remembered all the information about the planet Oldeira," the computer answered. "The CPU malfunction seems to have repaired itself."

Magnus frowned. "I don't like the sound of that. Something that can appear that suddenly and disappear even more suddenly is very untrustworthy. Go up to orbit and make sure of the diagnosis. When you find out what caused the problem, let us know."

Alea breathed a sigh of relief. For a moment, she'd been afraid she'd have to go back to her gilded prison. The caress of the night wind on her cheek seemed even sweeter.

"I shall do as you say," Herkimer said, "as soon as you are out of range of my sensors."

"Good idea," Gar said. "Let me know how you're doing."

"I shall," the computer said. "Good hunting."

Its infrared sensors watched as its humans crossed the meadow and disappeared into the trees. It waited a moment longer.

Actually, it waited quite a few moments, enough to make up several minutes, enough for a huge-headed, stumpy-legged, cat-like alien to waddle down the gangway and follow the humans into the forest. Herkimer wasn't aware of the delay, though, since Evanescent used her projective telepathy to make him forget everything from the moment the alien appeared in his field of vision until she vanished into the shadows beneath the trees.

The time wasn't forgotten so much as edited out—and this time, the alien remembered to reset Herkimer's clock so that the spaceship wouldn't know it had lingered more than a few seconds longer than it had to.

Then it was up and gone, rising on pressor beams until it was safe to use atmospheric drive. Up it spun into the stars, a disk of darkness against the splendor of the heavens, until it rose out of the shadow of the planet into the light of the sun and seemed one more star itself.

Gar and Alea didn't see, of course. They were already under the canopy of leaves, searching for a smaller clearing where they could pitch camp and light a fire.

Evanescent, though, found the nearest thicket and bedded down. She had no need to shadow her humans; she could follow their thoughts and find them whenever she wanted. Not that she intended to let them get too far ahead, of course. She wanted to stay close enough to get in on the fun.

Magnus and Alea kindled a fire and settled down for the night. Gar claimed first watch, but Alea was too excited to sleep. After half an hour of trying, she gave up and came to join him by the fire.

"What do you make of their clothing?" she asked Gar.

"I'd guess it's homemade versions of what was everyday wear on Terra, from back when their ancestors left to colonize this planet," he answered. "Probably looser to give more freedom of movement—after all, most of the city people did their work at desks, and when they did want to work out, they wore special exercise suits."

"Even the broad-brimmed hats?"

Magnus shrugged. "They're practical—keep the sun out of your eyes and the rain out of your face. Their coats, though, those are what interest me."

"Why?" Alea asked. "Their being hip length shows it doesn't get terribly cold, but that's about all—unless you mean the patterns."

"I do," Gar said. "It's as good as livery to show which side you're on."

"Yes, I suppose when you're fighting people your own size, you do need some way to tell friends from enemies." Alea came from a normal-sized people whose hereditary enemies were giants and dwarves. "Those sort of patterns look easy for weavers to make. I'm surprised there are so many variations, though."

"A people called Scots wove such plaids on old Earth," Gar mused. "They called them 'tartans.' When their history became fashionable, people pretended every clan had invented its own tartan."

"They didn't really, though?"

"It wasn't cast in iron," Magnus said, "nothing to prevent one clan from using cloth with a dozen different patterns—or none. Still, these people seem to have heard of the idea."

"They might," Alea said, "or they might have invented it on their own. It would be a natural thing for a weaver to hit upon, after all—bright, attractive, and not terribly difficult."

"That's true," Gar said thoughtfully. "I suppose these people don't have to be descended from Scots at all."

Alea frowned, looking closely at him. "There's another reason you think so, isn't there?"

Magnus sighed. "The Scots had a reputation for feuding, and that would explain all those skirmishes we saw on the screen as we orbited the planet."

"Feuding? What tribal society didn't?" Alea demanded. "I've been reading your history books. All your peoples had feuds before they settled down to farming. Some kept it going after that, too."

"Yes, and it's bad enough when people only have swords and axes," Magnus said. "These people, though, all have rifles."

"Appalling." Alea shuddered. "Absolutely appalling number of casualties. Thank Thor they take so long to reload!"

"Maybe we just came along when they happened to be at war," Gar said. "Maybe it doesn't really go on all the time."

"We can hope," Alea said darkly. "After all, if it does go on all the time, what can we do to stop it?"

"Oh, we'll think of something," Gar said softly.

Alea gave him a sharp look; his face had turned dreamy, and she could hear his thoughts clicking into place. If he couldn't start a revolution this time, he'd settle for bringing peace.

Somehow, she had a notion that this trip wouldn't be wasted.

Gar yielded the watch to her, slept four hours, then took up his vigil again—which was just as well, because the excitement had finally worn off, and Alea managed a few hours' sleep.

"A nap is better anyway," she told him over their breakfast of journeybread and coffee. "We'd only been awake ten hours when we landed."

"It will take a day or two to turn our inner rhythms around," Gar agreed. "Well, let's see what this planet holds, shall we?"

They drowned and buried the fire, then went off down lanes of fir trees with very little underbrush to impede them. The sun hadn't risen yet, and the forest was still filled with gloom—light enough to see where they were going, but dark enough to be dusk more than day.

"What's that glow in the air ahead?" Alea asked.

"Probably a rotten tree gone phosphorescent," Gar said, and changed course toward the luminous cloud. They'd only gone another dozen steps before he stopped dead, staring. "It can't be!"

Alea's eyes were wider than his. "It is!"

The cloud moved toward them with the angry hum of a dozen wings. The foot-high humanoids hovered before them, six-foot spans of gauzy wings forming a semicircular wall around the humans, some with arms folded, some with hands on hips, but all with fists, their faces glowing with anger.

2

W hy come you hither, mortals?" the foremost demanded.
"Your mind what madness fills?"

They looked as humans might have if they had evolved from
flying cats, very small cats with very large wings. Pointed ears
poked out of flowing manes atop their heads, the only hair on
their bodies. Their eyes were large with vertical pupils, noses
small and triangular, mouths lipless. Below the leaves and flowers that served them as clothing, their legs hung flexed by powerful thighs and calves.

"Know you not that the deep forests are ours?" the leader
demanded. "Are not the rolling meadows and the woodlands
enough for you?"

"Actually, we're strangers who don't know our way," Alea
said. "We have traveled far, and didn't know your customs."

"Traveled far! Whence upon this world can you have come
and not known of us?"

"Your ancestors crowded into this land unasked," another
fairy said, eyes bright with anger. "Ours were loathe to wreak ill
upon others, so they retreated from the coming of the strangers,
then retreated again—but when the human folk began to bring

their golden sickles deep within our forests in search of the oaks and mistletoe whose seed they had themselves brought, we cried 'Enough!' and taught them our anger."

"Have you no teachers," the first fairy asked, "that you have not learned what harm the wrath of the fair folk can bring?"

"I have heard a few stories, yes," Gar said slowly.

"And do you intend as much harm to us as others of your kind have wreaked upon one another?"

"We most surely do not!" Alea said indignantly.

"What of your mate?" another fairy demanded.

Alea colored. "He is not my mate!"

"It is as she says," Gar said with a sigh. "Nonetheless, I intend no harm to your kind either."

"But to your own?"

"I never intend harm, no," Gar said carefully.

The leader frowned. "Surely you do not say that you do harm without intending it!"

"When I am attacked, I defend myself—and when I see others oppressed, I defend them," Gar explained.

"So say all your kind," spat another fairy. "Nonetheless, they lie in wait for their enemies and strike them dead with their stinking smoke-tubes! What manner of defense is this—to ward yourself before they can think to strike you? Can you truly call that—"

"Softly, Cailleach," the leader said in an undertone.

Gar held his face steady to hide his recognition of the word. "Cailleach" meant "hag," and the third fairy was indeed more pale than the others, its skin wrinkled, but it bore no other signs of age—nor of gender, come to that.

"Her point is well taken, though," the leader said. "What assurance can you give that you will not 'defend' yourselves against us before we strike?"

"Their assurances would be meaningless, Ichorba," Cailleach snapped. "What they say when they are only two to our twenty, and what they will do if they come upon one of us alone, may not be . . ." Her head snapped up; she looked off to her right with a puzzled frown.

So did the rest of the troupe—except Ichorba. "So you have a guardian spirit." He was silent a moment, pupils dilating, then shrinking again. "You are avouched."

Then they were gone in a flurry of huge gauzy wings, shooting up among the limbs of the trees, darting into coverts, a few gliding away between trunks, their glow lighting a long avenue between trees.

Gar and Alea stood silent a moment, staring after them, dumbfounded. Then Alea breathed a sigh and said, "Well! All praise to our guardian spirit! Who is it, Gar?"

"I haven't the faintest idea," Gar said. "Unless it's Herkimer—but I've never known him to be telepathic."

"I didn't hear any thoughts."

"Neither did I, but the fair folk certainly did." Gar started forward again but held his staff in both hands, keenly alert. "It would seem we've been adopted by a local intelligent life-form."

"That would explain it," Alea said dubiously, "and would explain why the fair folk accepted its vouching for us. After all, I would guess they're native to this planet, too."

"They certainly don't look like Terran imports." Gar nodded. "Five centuries of evolution can't make all that great a change."

"Extra limbs would take considerably longer to grow," Alea agreed. "Their remote ancestor must have had six limbs for them to have been able to free two for wings."

"We'll have to keep an eye on the local wildlife," Gar said, "that is, assuming it hasn't all been exterminated by the birds and beasts the colonists brought with them."

"That's been known to happen." Alea had been cramming history, Terran and colonial. "Placental mammals wiped out most of the marsupials in Australia."

"I don't think these are mammals," Gar said. "At least, I didn't see any evidence of mammary glands."

Alea shrugged. "Nature is under no obligation to produce the same life-forms on every planet. For all we know, they lay eggs."

"Or reproduce by fission." Gar nodded. "No matter how they do, though, they're clearly native. *We're* the aliens here."

"Yes, and they're not too happy about it," Alea said grimly. "Do you think their ancestors really did retreat to make room for the colonists?"

"I suspect there was some fighting that their legends have conveniently forgotten," Gar said, echoing her grimness, "or maybe even outright extermination. Still, they could be remembering accurately that they didn't start fighting until people started invading their final sanctuary. By the way, what did you think about the Earthlings coming into the deep woods to search for oaks and mistletoe?"

"With golden sickles? They sound like Druids," Alea answered.

"They could well be," Gar said. "Maybe the original colonists were neo-Druids, looking for a place to set up a Celtic world."

"Not much chance of that back on Earth anymore," Alea agreed.

"Of course, we don't carry golden sickles," Gar said, "but I can see that the fair folk might have become nervous about any Earthlings coming into their domain."

"Serves us right for landing in the deep woods! And we thought it would keep people from noticing us."

"It did," Gar said. "Human people, anyway."

"Those fairy folk were as human as any of us," Alea said flatly. "From now on, we should talk about our own kind as Earthlings."

"That's fair enough."

"No, *they* are."

"Well, no, they didn't actually *say* they were fairies," Gar pointed out. "Still, if we hear Earthlings use the word, we'll know we're up against something more than superstition. I wonder what kind of trouble they thought they could make?"

"We'll have to ask to hear the local version of fairy tales," Alea said, "when we find some people—Earthlings, I mean."

"At any rate, we won't have to worry about the fairies making trouble for us," Gar said.

"Yes, since they seem to trust our guardian, whatever that is."

"That *is* something we can worry about," Gar said. "When and where did we acquire a guardian spirit?"

"And how?" Alea shrugged. "Maybe we have an aura of good intentions about us."

"Intentions, yes," Gar said with a wry smile. "I'm not always so sure about my *accomplishments.*"

Alea glanced up at him with a frown. It wasn't the first time she'd heard him make disparaging comments about himself. How could so valiant and gentle a man not think well of himself? More to the point, how did it affect the way he dealt with her? She decided she'd have to work on it.

The fairies must have been overly sensitive, or the forests not as extensive as they had once been, for they came out of the trees to find the sun newly risen. A broad meadow stretched before them. They followed a deer track to a river; they knew it was a deer track because they saw a doe with two fawns.

"More immigrants." Gar nodded toward the animals.

"Druids would have brought deer, I suppose," Alea agreed.

They followed the river for an hour before they came to a dirt road, tilting downward to the shallows.

"Roads mean people," Alea said. "Which way?"

Gar shrugged. "One is as good as another, and I don't feel like getting my feet wet."

They followed the road up the riverbank, under trees vivid with falling leaves of red and gold, between fields guarded by split-rail fences, raw with the stubble of harvest and dotted with the upside down cones of corn shocks.

"Fall here, I'd guess," Alea said.

"They do seem to be good farmers."

"And herders." Alea pointed her staff at some cows wandering out of a grove to graze in a field off to their right.

"All we need now are their owners," Gar said.

"You've found them," said a deep gravelly voice.

Out of the woods stepped three people in broad-brimmed hats and loose trousers, their coats in grids of green and yellow. Three more like them rose from a ditch on the other side of the road. This close, Gar and Alea could see that some wore close-cropped beards without mustaches, while others were smooth-faced. Some of the beardless ones were clearly young men, others were clearly women.

All carried long flintlock rifles, every one of which seemed to be aimed at himself and Alea.

"That's a tartan I don't know," said the eldest, a graybeard. "Where are you from, strangers, and what's your clan?"

They both knew that the truth was best. "I'm a Pike from Maxima, and my companion is a Larsdatter," Gar told him.

"Never heard of 'em." The man eyed him with suspicion. "Where's this Maxima?"

"Far away," Gar told him. "Very far away."

"Sure must be," a young man said. "We've never heard of it!"

"You leave the talking to those who're grown enough to have some wisdom, Jethro," the graybeard said, never taking his eyes from Gar and Alea.

"Oh, all right, Uncle Isaac," Jethro said, but he still glowered at Gar.

"He's got a point, though," said Uncle Isaac. "You must've come hundreds of miles."

"You understand me well," Gar said, nodding. "I can't go home until I've found what I'm looking for."

"Oh." Jethro lowered his rifle. "We understand about wander-years."

"Don't usually send our young folks off without full guard, though," Uncle Isaac said suspiciously.

"It was my choice," Gar said evenly, "and mine not to come home, if misfortune befell me."

Gun barrels lowered amid exclamations of distress and sympathy.

"What was it, then, lad?" one young woman asked, eyes wide. "What hurt—"

"His business and none other's!" said an older woman. "Ours not to pry, youngling."

The young woman clamped her jaw shut, but her eyes burned with resentment.

"What of her, then?" A young man gave Alea a weighing glance that turned to a gleam.

"Indeed," said Uncle Isaac. "What of you, young woman?"

"I am the last of my clan," Alea said stiffly.

The clansfolk stared, and several voices murmured with sympathy.

"Ah well, no wonder you're far from your birthplace, then!" said a woman whose hair was streaked with gray.

"You come home with us and get some food in your bellies," said another woman with lustrous brown hair and only a few lines in her face. "Poor lass, you must be near starved."

"She's skinny enough," said the young man with the hot eyes.

Gar turned to him with a smile that became a grin.

"Keep your eyes to yourself and your own, Eli," the gray-haired woman snapped.

"As you say, Aunt Martha," the young man said reluctantly.

"I do say! No call for you to go looking elsewhere, with your Aura Lee to come home to." Aunt Martha stepped forward, reaching out to Alea. "You come on along now, child. We'll make you a pallet, and if it's on the floor, at least it will be indoors and by a fire! How long's it been since you slept with a roof over your head?"

"Her neighbors surely weren't about to take her in," one young woman said to another in a low voice.

"Aye, staying near when your clan is killed is inviting death," her friend agreed.

"Sure is," Jethro said. "It's the same as being outlawed."

Expressions turned startled, then wary. Rifle barrels rose again.

"Jethro, I told you to leave the talking to those as have some sense!" Uncle Isaac blustered.

"Sole survivor's only an outlaw if she's close to home," the brown-haired woman told Jethro scornfully.

"Well, she's a woman, though," Jethro grumbled. "Why hasn't she married into another clan? If she's journeyed so far, she's had plenty of chances."

"Maybe none of 'em any more comely than you, though!" a young woman said, wrinkling her nose.

"Right enough, Sukey," the brown-haired woman said, and to Jethro, "Could be she didn't fall in love, you know."

"Oh, didn't she?" Jethro jerked his head at Gar. "Why's she traveling with him, then?"

"Because she can trust me," Gar told him, "and it's safer to travel with a partner. But romance? Look at me, lad. Is this the kind of face to win a woman's love?"

Jethro locked glares with him—so Gar didn't see the longing look Alea gave him, quickly masked, nor the kindling glances of the younger clanswomen.

"No," Jethro said with a contemptuous sneer. "Only a mother could love that face."

"Handsome is as handsome does, fool!" Sukey jibed.

"Then you must've done ugly work," Jethro told Gar.

"Ugly indeed," Gar agreed, "as any fool could tell you."

Jethro's sneer vanished. "Why a fool?"

"Because it would take a fool to call him out," Uncle Isaac said, "a man that size."

"Without a rifle?"

"Guns are for cowards." Gar lifted his staff. "Any man with real courage would come at me with nothing more than this."

"There's truth in that, lad," Aunt Martha said slowly, "but there's folly, too. If you're crossing a meadow and a Belinkun shoots at you, you'd best not go chasing him with nothing but a stick or he'll shoot you dead."

"If he has time to reload," Gar said, his gaze locked with Jethro's.

"Them Belinkuns never goes out alone," Jethro said with scorn. "That's almost as much folly as not carrying a rifle."

"Why, so it is," Gar said softly, "and now you'll understand why the young lady travels with me even though we're not in love."

Jethro's face went slack with surprise at the argument's going full circle. The young women laughed.

"He's got you there, Jethro!"

"He beat you by good sense!"

Jethro reddened with embarrassment and anger.

"There's no losing when people manage to make one another understand," Gar said, "only winning—on both sides."

Jethro looked even more surprised at being offered a way to save face. Then he gave a bitter laugh. "Tell that to the Belinkun clan!"

"Why, so I shall," Gar said, speaking softly again, "if you'll point me the way and give me a safe-conduct through your lands."

The clan stared at him in surprise. Then Uncle Isaac laughed, stepping forward to clap him on the shoulder. "I believe you'd do it, too! But it would be the death of you, stranger; those Belinkuns are treacherous as snakes and twice as deadly!"

"I've dealt with snakes before," Gar said evenly.

"Yes, but those snakes weren't carrying rifles."

Alea didn't realize she'd grown tense until she relaxed. She turned to the young women, lifting an eyebrow in exasperation. "Now that the bulls have stopped pawing the ground, maybe we can talk clearly to one another."

"I always did like to watch a good bullfight," Aunt Martha

said with a grin. She put an arm around Alea's shoulders. "You come home with us now, lass, and maybe we can get the men to be civil long enough to eat dinner."

The travelers thought they were still among fields when a minor mob burst caroling from a grove.

"Daddy! Did you shoot me a deer?"

"Mama, Mama! What's for dinner?"

"Uncle Silas, did you fight another bear?"

"Mommy, did you shoot me that new hat?"

"No, dear." The brown-haired woman ruffled a little boy's hair with a fond smile. "The raccoons don't come out till night."

"They might have stepped out in the daylight just to oblige you," Jethro said, "but this big galoot scared 'em away, he's so ugly."

The children saw the strangers and fell silent, their eyes growing round.

"Why, thank you, Jethro," Gar said with a smile. "It's nice to be given my due."

"He's a giant!" a little girl said.

"So's she!" A ten-year-old pointed to Alea.

"Molly," Aunt Martha said severely, "it's not polite to point." Molly stuck her hands behind her back but kept staring.

Alea smiled. "Don't worry, little one. You're not the first to say it." She tried to ignore the bitterness of the memories.

"That's enough, now," Aunt Martha said. "You leave the guests alone till they've had a chance to wash up and rest a little." She turned one of the boys around and gave him a little push. "Go tell Great Grandma, now, and the others."

"Sure, Gammy!" the boy cried, and took off. The juvenile score ran howling behind him to spread the word to their contemporaries.

"They wander far," Alea said.

"Not so far as all that." Gammy beckoned and walked onward. They went down the road another rod and turned into a lane. Alea stared; the roadside thicket had hidden a four-foot-high wall of fieldstone. A gate of oak sheathed with brass closed the lane, but it was open and a clansman stood by it grinning, his rifle pointing at the ground. "Good hunting, folks?"

"Only these, Hiram." Uncle Isaac held up a brace of partridge. Another held up a pair of rabbits and a third several more partridges. "And these." He nodded toward Gar and Alea.

"Big game indeed!" the gatekeeper said, grinning wider. "The tads told me you were bringing a giant, but I didn't believe them."

"I prefer to think of myself as a bonus," Gar said.

"A bonus to any clan that has you, I'd say! Can you shoot?"

Gar shrugged. "Well enough, I suppose, but I'd rather fight hand to hand."

"Well, then, I hope you don't meet any bears!" Hiram grinned and waved as they went on through.

Alea halted with a gasp of surprise. "It's a manor house! I'd never have known it was here."

"Of course not," Gammy said. "We wouldn't want the Belinkuns to be able to see at a glance how many were home, would we?"

The clan's house was a great rambling three-story structure with wings added on at each side, then at right angles, and finally forming a square, as generations had toiled to make more living space. Even so, they had finally outgrown the ancestral mansion, because smaller houses formed a semicircle in front of the big one. The ground between was a luxuriant lawn landscaped with concentric beds of flowers separated by graveled walks. Wherever the clan fought its battles, it had managed to keep them away from home.

Their hosts led Gar and Alea up the widest gravel walk to the massive front door of the mansion.

A blood-curdling shriek pierced the air.

3

Alea whirled to see a dozen children of various ages come hurtling around the corner of the house. Another band sprang howling from the shade of a great old willow.

"Belinkuns!" several voices shouted. "Get 'em!"

The children leveled wooden rifles and shouted "Bang! Boom!" and other assorted noises. Some spun about with harrowing cries and fell in very theatrical death scenes. In two minutes, only two children were left standing on each side.

"No fair, Clay!" one girl called. "I shot you!"

"Can't have, Lizzy!" a boy called back. "Farlands always win, you know that."

Lizzy pouted but dutifully sank down and threw herself about in very loud death throes. So did her compatriot.

"Battle's over," one of the survivors declared.

The corpses jumped up, and Lizzy called, "I want to be a Farland this time!"

"Yeah, Clay!" a boy called. "Your turn to be a Belinkun!"

"Turnabout is fair, Clay," Jethro called.

Clay heaved a massive sigh and lifted his toy rifle. "Okay, I'm Hezekiah Belinkun!"

"No, I'm Hezekiah," a tall girl said. "I'm the oldest."

"Hezekiah's a man, though," Clay objected.

"Well then, I'll be Great Gran Belinkun," the girl stated. "Okay, Hezekiah, call up the clan! The sentries are telling us them Farlands are attacking!"

Alea stared, then exchanged a quick glance with Gar and saw the same horror in his eyes as she felt in her heart.

"Welcome to our house," Gammy said formally.

"Thank you," Gar said, his face a smooth mask again. He turned and scraped his boot across a dull blade set beside the door, then scraped the other and went into the house. Alea imitated his actions, wondering how he had known about the boot-scraper, and followed him in.

The first thing that struck Alea was the number of children running around the place. She would have thought that the mock battle she'd seen included all of the younger generation, but there were at least that many more playing intricate games with balls and tiny hoops, setting plates and forks on the long table in the center of the hall, or roughhousing with a great old patient sheepdog who lay near the hearth. Her amazement subsided a little and she had time to notice the room itself. It was huge, with a ten-foot ceiling and wainscoting of a golden wood. Between wainscot and ceiling, the plaster was whitewashed and hung with a dozen or more pictures, portraits, and landscapes done with varying degrees of skill, but all warm in tone and expressing a feeling of safety.

Alea realized that the clansfolk had fashioned a refuge, a retreat to give them the feeling of a security they might not have had in real life.

"Jeb will take you out back to the pump," Gammy said. "When you've freshened up a bit, we'll introduce you to Great Grandma."

"We'll look forward to it," Alea said, then turned to follow a young man across the great room to a door in the hearth wall.

• • •

Behind it was a bathroom, which was to say, a room for taking a bath. A great tub of gray metal stood at one end, and beside it was a stove with a huge kettle hanging from a stout boom. Alea realized that the stove shared the chimney with the fireplace in the main room. At the other end of the chamber was a row of windows. Beneath them stood a counter with a large basin, a small pump perched beside it.

Alea frowned, recognizing the machine from her reading. She went forward and worked the handle warily, but sure enough, gouts of water sprang from the spout into the basin. "You too, traveler," she called to Gar. "Take off a layer of dust or two."

Gar laid his hat on the counter and came up beside her to splash water on his face. Jeb handed them each a towel. Drying her face, Alea looked out the window before her and saw four small outbuildings in a row. She remembered more reading and recognized them as privies.

Jeb took her towel and hung it on a nearby rack. "How about a slice of bread and a hunk of cheese, with some cider to wash it down?"

Alea was suddenly aware that she was hungry. "That would be good, but isn't it nearly dinnertime? It smells wonderful."

"Almost ready," Jeb agreed.

"We'd just be in the way in the kitchen, then," Alea told him. "I think we're ready to meet Great Grandma—if she's ready for us."

Jeb glanced questioningly at Gar, but he nodded, so Jeb said, "I reckon she's ready. Let's go."

He led them out the door and down the length of the room. Alea saw that the table was fully set now, with a loaf of bread near each end. In the massive chair at the table's head sat an ancient woman, bony and spare of frame, face lined and cheeks sunken with age, but the eyes that met Alea's were bright with intelligence and lively with curiosity. She sat erect as a pine and wore a dark blue dress with a white lace collar and cuffs. Uncle

Isaac stood near her, shifting his weight from side to side and frowning with concern.

"Oh, quit hovering, Isaac!" the old woman told him. "I'm not about to kick off in the next minute or two. Cease your fluttering and introduce me to these nice people."

"If you say so, Aunt Emily," Isaac said, not reassured. He came around to the guests and held out a hand. "Gar Pike and Alea Larsdatter, this is Emily Farland, Great Grandmother of our clan."

"Please to meet you." Alea couldn't help curtsying, awed by the woman's age.

Gar followed her example with a little bow. "It is an honor to make your acquaintance, Ms. Farland."

"Say 'missus' clear, lad," Great Grandmother Farland said severely. "None of this mumbling, now. I hope you insist your man treats you like a lady, Alea Larsdatter."

"Oh, he does, ma'am," Alea said, "but he's not mine."

"I am your friend, I hope," Gar said gravely.

"Well, yes, and the closest I've ever had," Alea said, her gaze imploring his understanding.

"But only a friend, hey?" Great Grandma asked. "Well, you'll learn the truth of it in time."

Alea hid her exasperation. Why was it that even total strangers thought she and Gar were bonded? Not that she minded the idea, of course, but . . .

She froze, shocked at herself. When had that notion crept in? Gar was a friend, a good friend even, but nothing more!

"Isaac tells me you've come a long way," the matriarch said, and to Alea, "My sympathies for your loss, lass."

"Thank you," Alea mumbled, then remembered the old woman chastising Gar and said clearly, "It's been two years and more, though, so I'm past the worst of it."

"Decided on living, have you? Well, it was the right choice." Great Grandma turned to Gar. "What set you on your travels, though, young man?"

"Heartbreak, I suppose you'd have to say," Gar said slowly. "Heartbreak of a kind."

Alea fought to keep her face impassive. That explained a good deal about him, but why had he never told her?

Because she had never asked, of course—she had to admit that. He had said it so openly, so readily, that he would surely have answered her, but it was too personal a question for her to have said aloud.

Not the way Great Grandma asked it, of course.

"Heartbreak," the old lady said, musing. "And you have to find a way to mend it before you can go home, eh?"

"That's . . . one way to say it," Gar said, a bit disconcerted.

Isaac laughed and clapped him on the shoulder. "That's why she's the clan chief, lad—'cause she can see right through you in an instant, man or woman."

"See right through a problem, too," Aunt Martha said, coming up, "whether it be a fight between two of her folk or a Belinkun attack, she sees the way to set it right in an instant."

"You're shaping up pretty well yourselves," said Great Grandma. "Both of you. When I kick off, I won't be leaving the clan lorn." She gave Alea a bright, challenging glance. "What trouble would you have me see through, girl?"

Alea stood stunned, then bit her tongue to keep from saying the first and most honest answer. Instead she said, "Why, the way for an orphan to find a home, Grandma Farland."

"An orphan, is it?" Great Grandma asked. "Well, the way of it is to find yourself a man and make a family of your own, girl, for you'll never be an orphan then."

"What if the man won't be found?" Alea was very much aware of Gar's gaze on her, amused and sympathetic at the same time—and altogether too interested.

"Then find out who your people are, even if you have to go all the way back to the Founders," Great Grandma said, "for surely no one comes to life alone, and every one of us is part of something greater. We all have kin, whether we know it or not. Distant they may be, but kin nonetheless."

Pain lanced Alea's heart, for she couldn't help but think of the third and fourth cousins who had gleefully cast her down into slavery when her parents died and no man had come forward to ask her hand. Her voice had an edge as she asked, "What if they be kin but won't have you?"

Great Grandma had already seen her pain, though, and her gaze had turned sympathetic. "Ah, then, poor child, you choose among the clans that will have you. Like will to like, as the poet says. Find them as are like to you and cleave unto them. Seek out the clan that will have you, and that you will have." One old wrinkled finger speared upward in caution. "But don't jump too fast. Bide with them a while and sound them out, for there be some as will have you only to use you, and only one or two that will have you because you're their kind."

Alea glanced at Gar, she couldn't help herself, but as quickly glanced away. "You're saying that the clan that are my kind will take me in even if they don't like me?"

"They will that, because, as the other poet says, when you have to go there, they have to take you in—that's what it means to be your kind. But unhappiness lies that way, child. Don't settle for half. Seek for likeness and liking both, and don't take less, though the searching takes you half your life. It will be worth it when you find it."

Alea stared, confounded. "How could you know?"

"Why," said Great Grandma with a warm and loving smile, "that was my own tale too, upon a time. I wasn't born to this clan, child. No woman is, for marrying cousins leads to madness or sickly children, or idiots who are children in bodies grown."

"Marriage to third and fourth cousins is allowed," Isaac said stiffly.

"Yes, and we all know your Dory is the love of your life and the life of your love, Isaac, though she be your third cousin once removed," Great Grandma said with a touch of exasperation, "but there aren't all of us that lucky." She turned back to Alea. "I went on wandertime with a band of my own clan, lass, and other bands joined us as we journeyed. My Tyler was among them, but I didn't say 'yes' to him till I'd stayed a month with his family, that I didn't, and made sure they were my kind and I theirs."

"No one could be more a Farland than you, Aunt Em," said Isaac.

"Yes, well, that's because there's scarce a one of you that isn't as much my flesh and blood as Tyler's, now, isn't it?" Great Grandma said. "It's a wonder what age and time can do. But his people was as much like me as my own, maybe more." She nodded with satisfaction. "I was lucky, that's a fact." She cocked an eye at Alea. "You will be too, child—wait and see."

"I'll wait." Alea gave Gar a very direct stare of her own. "You never have taken me to meet your people."

"It's a long way home," Gar said apologetically.

"Help him find the poultice that will heal his heart, child," Great Grandma advised. "Then follow him home and see if his kind are your kind, and one among them more than a friend."

Alea suddenly realized which one of them she wanted to be more than a friend, but fear clamored up with desire and left her mute.

Great Grandma turned toward the kitchen with a frown. "The body goes and the senses weaken, but I could swear I smell pork chops cooking."

"So you do, and they're ready to serve," Aunt Martha said, coming up. "Sukey bade me call us all to table, Gran. You're there, I see, and the guests."

"Go beat the triangle, then, Martha," Great Grandma said. "Just be sure it's not the alarm bell."

It looked like the great hall of a medieval castle, a double rank of tables made of plank tops set on sawhorses, covered with linen and set with wooden plates and bowls with whittled spoons and forks. The clansfolk cut with their belt knives and drank from pottery mugs. The great keeping room was alive with laughter and jesting, with here and there the wailing of a baby. Great

Grandma sat through it all, eyes gleaming with pride, eating little but nodding with satisfaction.

The conversation ranged widely; the great room was filled with a hum of talk. Very little of it involved Great Grandma, though. Now and again one or two of the clansfolk would come up to her with a disagreement and ask her for fact or opinion. She always told them the straight of it without hesitation; they always went away, satisfied.

"Strange how it's so often the great grandmother who leads the clan," Gar said to Isaac, who sat across the table from him at Great Grandma's right hand. Gar even kept a straight face through Alea's mental jibe: *So often? As though we'd visited a hundred clans?*

"That's because the women live longer than the men." Isaac nodded sagely.

"Can we help it if our constitutions are stronger?" asked Martha. "We take our share of risks when the Belinkuns attack, you know!"

"Oh, I know it well," Isaac assured her. "Still, I've heard of clans where it was the great grandfather who was clan chief—until he died, of course."

"Well, you can't be surprised if the younger folk turn to his wife for comfort and guidance then, Isaac," Grandma Em said. "After all, we've lived so much longer than you that we're bound to know better what to do." She sighed, shaking her head. "I'm growing weary, though—weary and weak. I'll be taking to my rocker soon, and letting one of you younger folk take the lead."

"As long as you're there to lead the leader, Gran," Martha said.

"Only when you truly have need of me," Grandma Em said. "Old folks grow tired, you know, Martha—tired and weak."

"But never dull," Isaac said. "You're still sharp as a razor, Gran."

Alea looked at his beard, glanced at the full bushes on the other men, and was surprised they even knew what a razor was.

When the meal was over and the children set to clearing away the dishes, several teenagers pulled the corks from jugs and went from place to place, pouring two fingers' worth into each mug. Alea tasted hers and felt fire burn all the way down into her stomach. She glanced at Gar and from the roundness of his eyes knew he was feeling the same. He exhaled loudly and said, "What a delightful aftertaste!"

Great Grandma nodded in pleasure. "That's my own recipe, that is—peaches in with the mash. The flavor grows as it goes through the still."

At one of the tables, a man began to sing. Others joined in, higher voices harmonizing with lower, some even high enough to send a descant floating over the music during the choruses. Gar and Alea listened in pleased amazement as the voices sang,

*"On Springfield Mountain
There did dwell
A handsome youth,
I knew him well.*

*"Too-roo-li-yay,
Too-roo-li-yoo,
Too-roo-li-yay,
Too-roo-li-yoo."*

The clansfolk told, with tongue in cheek, how the handsome youth had been bitten by a snake and how his true love had tried to save him by sucking out the poison but had finished by dying with him. When it was done, Gar and Alea sat amazed, partly by the beauty of the singing, but also by the spirit in which the story had been told—and by the spirits in their mugs, but they sipped sparingly at those.

"What of yourselves, travelers?" Isaac asked. "Can you offer song in return?"

"Time to sing for our suppers," Gar muttered to Alea.

Alea bit her lip, trying furiously to remember the song of

the Lorelei, but Gar turned to his hosts and said, "I'll be glad to sing, Goodman Isaac, if you'll suffer the cawing of a crow." Then he began to sing in a surprisingly rich baritone,

> "Now East is East and West is West,
> And never the twain shall meet . . ."

Alea listened, amazed, to the tale of a horse thief and the young man who chased him, ending with the young man riding the stolen horse home with the thief's son beside him. She hadn't known Gar could sing so well and wondered why he never had before.

She wasn't so caught up in his song, though, as to miss its effect on the clansfolk. They followed the tale of the chase with excitement, cheered the young man's defiance when the thief had him at his mercy, then turned thoughtful as the two declared their respect for one another and the young man pledged friendship with the thief's son. She decided Gar had chosen an interesting selection for a clan dedicated to a feud.

They learned quickly, though. As he began to sing the first verse again, to end the song, several of the clansfolk joined in. When he finished, they applauded, and Great Grandma Em nodded. "A good song, young man, and one so long merits another in return. Tull, sing the 'Lay of the Founders' for us."

A young man rose, reddening, and said, "If you please, Gran, but I'll ask everyone else to join in when they should."

"Of course, lad," said Isaac. "On with the song, then."

Tull cleared his throat and began.

> "When Old Earth had sickened with surfeit,
> Her people with envy beset,
> All their needs satisfied, all their wants magnified,
> Buying baubles though burdened with debt.
> When character rotted with people besotted
> Their only watchword being 'Get!'

"With envy corrupted and morals bankrupted,
Caring only for pleasure and wealth,
Their ambition self-seeking, with greed and lust reeking,
Devoted to nothing but Self.

"Then rose up in alarm Jed and Laura the Farlands,
Seeking clean air for family and brood.
They called up their clan, every woman and man,
And said, 'Let us go where we all know we should.'

"The clan answered . . ."

"Aye!" all the clansfolk responded with a massed shout that shook the walls.

Tull went on without missing a beat.

". . . and pledged to raise high,
To alien breezes unfurled,
Their clan flag on some other world.

"They sold what they could, labored all for clan's good,
Earning cash to provision a ship . . ."

The lay went on for half an hour. Alea was staggered not only by its length and the amount of detail, but also by the verve with which the clansfolk shouted their responses, by their total devotion to the goals of their ancestors—even when those goals became murderous.

For the Farlands weren't the only people who had decided to give their unborn children a clean start. So had many other families, though the song implied that the Farlands had led the way in their own spaceship and the others had simply followed along to steal the clan's real estate. Alea had read enough about terraforming and genetics to know that couldn't be true, that it would have taken hundreds of thousands of people to tame an alien world and seed it with Terran plants and animals, even with the help of robots and automated farming equipment. Moreover, she knew that those hundreds of thousands of people would have had to raise millions in cash to be able to buy those machines, not to mention the seeds and the animal embryos to stock their farms.

Apparently they had also brought along rifles.

Whatever organization had remained on Terra to earn money and ship them supplies, was disbanded when a reactionary government came to power on the home world and cut off all the colony planets that weren't self-supporting. Claiming that the colonists were impoverishing Terra, the reactionaries only kept up relations with the older colony worlds, the ones that had been established so long that they were able to export raw materials to Terra for its orbital factories, and to buy the goods those factories produced.

Suddenly tractors became fabulously precious. Shortly after, they became useless because there was no fuel. People began to plow with oxen again. The forgotten hay rakes and reapers were reconstructed from history books, farmers learned how to use scythes again, and people reinvented the wagon wheel. Agriculture staggered on, but without pesticides or fertilizers, save manure, and yields dropped dramatically.

Livestock could graze the marginal lands that weren't fit for tilling, so sheep, goats, and especially cows became vital to survival—which meant that bulls also became important. Most were gelded to make draft animals or meat, of course; each clan kept only one or two of the strongest and most massive for breeding.

Then the Belinkuns' bull died. Faced with no new calves and knowing the Farlands had prudently kept two bulls, they organized a midnight raid and stole a Farland bull.

That, of course, was a life-threatening action, since there was no guarantee the remaining bull would prove potent in the spring. There was recourse, though, and Rogan, the clan chief, sent a dozen clansfolk to the High Druid to petition for justice. The party had a great deal of difficulty getting there; the roads had deteriorated sadly since the enchanted machines that built and repaired them had expired. The Farlands' magic chariot kept breaking down and needing new spells, but there were few wizards to re-enchant it and get it going again.

Finally, though, they did come to the High Druid and laid their case before him. He gave them his judgment; the price of the bull must be a hundred cows and the first bull calf of the next season. He wrote that judgment on paper in magical runes and gave it to the Farlands to take and show to the Belinkuns, but he could send no guards to enforce the penalty; all his men had gone home to farm, since they could no longer be fed from the surplus that Homeworld magic had created.

The enchantment on the Farlands' chariot had now worn off completely, so they had to walk home. The clan rejoiced at the judgment and went as a body to present the High Druid's letter to the Belinkuns.

They brought their rifles, of course. No one ever went anywhere without one in those days. There were snakes to kill, and always a chance of a rabbit or even a wild pig for dinner.

Rogan laid the High Druid's judgment before the Belinkuns. Orbin, the leader of the party who had gone to the High Druid, recited his threats of supernatural punishment for the Belinkuns if they disobeyed his edict.

They laughed.

Worse, they mocked the High Druid and jeered at the notion that he had any authority to judge them. Worst of all, they mocked Rogan. Angered, he struck Enoch—the Belinkun leader—slapped him across both cheeks, then turned on his heel and strode away.

A ratcheting sounded behind, the noise of flintlocks being cocked, and many of the Farlands glanced backward dubiously, lifting their own rifles—but Rogan strode angrily onward, never glancing back, and his people turned to follow him, each expecting at any moment to feel a rifle ball in their backs. Enoch bade his people not to fire, though, for he would not have it said that he was so cowardly as to attack his enemy from behind.

It was the last time such honor was observed between the clans.

Outraged at the Belinkuns' impiety and even more at their insolence, the Farlands attacked in force and stole their bull back—leaving half a dozen Belinkuns dead and carrying home two corpses of their own. Each clan hated the other as murderers, and the stolen bull's price had been increasing for centuries, paid in the blood and life of clansfolk.

When the song was done, Gar and Alea sat stunned while the clansfolk cheered around them.

"Well sung," Grandma Em judged, nodding with satisfaction. "He's a rare fine singer, our Tull."

"It always feels good, being reminded why we're fighting." Martha drank off the last of her ale and stood up. "But the morning doesn't start any later just because we have guests. May I help you to your bedroom, Aunt?"

"Yes, thank you, Martha." Grandma Em stood without assistance, though both Isaac and Martha sprang close to catch her if they were needed. "I've managed," she told them with an impish smile, then turned to nod graciously to her guests. "Thank you for your song."

"It was our pleasure," Gar said.

"The least we could do to repay such excellent hospitality," Alea added.

"Isaac will show you to your rooms." Grandma Em turned away, leaning heavily on Martha's arm and on her cane. "Sleep well."

"Sleep well," Gar and Alea replied, "and thanks."

They watched the old lady hobble away, then turned to Isaac who said, "Come. I'll show you where to sleep."

They lay awake in small whitewashed rooms surrounded by darkness, but their thoughts sounded in each other's minds.

How much of that story was fact, Alea wondered, *and how much fiction?*

Legends do turn into better stories as the years pass, and they're told and retold, Gar admitted, *but there's always a core of fact. One thing we know is true—that when the PEST party came to power on Terra, it did indeed cut off commerce and aid to the colony planets.*

Alea nodded, though she knew he could not see. *And I think it's not too unlikely that whatever kind of central government this colony had, just withered up and died without Terran money and equipment to keep it going.*

Certainly it would have lost communication with the towns and villages, Gar agreed, *when the road-repairing equipment ran out of gas and spare parts, and the radios and computers broke down and couldn't be fixed.*

The dwarves of Midgard learned how to make their own. Alea couldn't hide a bit of gloating when she found something to be said in favor of her home planet.

Gar took it as a good sign. *Not all colonies were lucky enough to have people who learned electronics so quickly—and you must admit the dwarves weren't big on road-building.*

Well, no, but the giants were. I take your point, though—there aren't any giants here, either.

They do seem to be excellent farmers, if the crops and orchards we've seen are anything to go by, Gar pointed out, *and skilled fighters, from what we saw in the satellite photos. Maybe that's why the central government had a system for resolving disputes between clans.*

Yes, a system headed by Druids. Alea frowned. *That's the only evidence of religion I've noticed around here.*

At least when the central government died, there was some form of law left, Gar said, *even if it was only religious law.*

The Druids were supposed to have been skilled as judges according to their own legal code. Alea had read the books more recently than Gar. *It only works as long as the people believe in the religion, though.*

Yes, and if Enoch Belinkun's reaction to the High Druid is any indication, these people had lost their faith pretty thoroughly, Gar said. *I find it in me to wonder how deeply their ancestors believed it.*

Just introduced it as a kind of play-acting, you mean? I think that's a little unjust, Alea said. *After all, every generation finds some belief of their own to prove their independence. Children and grandchildren could have drifted farther and farther away from the Druids' teachings.*

Away from Druidism—but toward what? Gar wondered. *What replaced it? What do they believe in now?*

The blood feud, Alea thought darkly. *The vendetta.*

Yes. Gar's thoughts had somber overtones. *When there's no law, people band together into clans and tribes for security. Their only protection against strangers' mayhem is knowing their own clan will take revenge if they're hurt.*

So someone from clan A kills someone from clan B, Alea said, *and clan B kills a clan A member in revenge.*

Then clan B goes out to kill as many clan A people as it can, Gar said. *Vengeance begets vengeance, and pretty soon clansfolk from A are killing clansfolk from B in revenge for the last death, and clansfolk B are killing clansfolk A in revenge for the revenge . . .*

. . . And revenge for the revenge for the revenge, Alea said, *and so on and so on and so on.*

Before long, A clansfolk are killing B clansfolk whenever they can, simply because they were born to, Gar finished, *and no one even remembers how it started.*

Or if they do, they don't care, Alea said. *Neither do I. Never mind how they started the feud—how do we stop it?*

By introducing law, Gar answered.

Brilliant, Professor, Alea thought with withering sarcasm. *How do you intend to do that?*

I haven't quite worked out that part yet, Gar admitted.

He would, though—Alea was sure of that. She felt a cold chill. Gar's plans always worked, but they sometimes had disastrous side effects.

The clansfolk were up bright and early—very bright, and far too early. They were out feeding the barnyard animals in the false dawn. When Gar and Alea were on the road, though, that was when they usually woke up, so they sat down with the family and pitched in to a very hearty breakfast.

They were at the head table again, and the talk was of the crops and the stock, the weather and the work to be done that day. Gar and Alea listened, soaking it all in but unable to join the conversation, since they knew nothing of the topics—not here, at least.

After a while, the family realized it, and an uneasy silence settled as everyone thought frantically of a topic that would include the guests, but Alea found one first, one that had been piquing her curiosity for some time. "We met some . . . people on the road such as we've never seen before—glowing creatures with wings who claimed to be older than any human folk. Could they have been real?"

Isaac and Martha shrank back in their chairs, making signs against evil. So did Grandma Em, but she gave them a look that was quite severe and demanded, "Had you gone into the deep woods, then? Tell me you didn't meet them in the fields!"

"No, we didn't," Alea stammered. "We lost our way . . ."

"In the woods." Gar took up the tale with easy grace. "The road led into a woodlot, then ended. We cast about, trying to find our way back to the fields, but the trees grew larger and larger until . . ."

"Grandma Em!" A young man hurried up to the table, rifle still in one hand as he snatched off his hat with the other. "Ephraim has sent word, from the fence out past the north forty. He saw the glitter off a gun barrel coming down the hillside a mile off. Then a flock of grackles burst into the air, making a racket that sounded an alarm for all the birds in the forest!"

4

An alarm for us, too!" Isaac shoved back his chair as he rose. "There's Belinkuns coming through them woods!" Then he remembered the courtesies and turned to Grandma Em. "Shall we go against them?"

"Do," Grandma said, "but only send twenty rifles. Leave a dozen here and have the other ten scout the rest of the boundaries. It's not like the Belinkuns to let themselves be seen so easy."

"Diversion!" Martha snapped. "They're trying to draw us away while their main body attacks somewhere else! You take the twenty, Isaac, and I'll go scout with the ten!"

"Sound the alarm," Isaac told the young man, who nodded and hurried away.

Word had run by itself through the keeping room, though. All the clansfolk were up and running for their weapons except for a few Grandma Em's age, who sat and swore because they were too old to do more than hug the little ones who stared, wide-eyed and frightened, as their parents and big brothers and big sisters rushed about, snatching up weapons and hats and bolting for the door. In minutes they were gone, leaving only the old and the young. Even the bigger children exclaimed in anger and pleaded with their seniors to be allowed to go out and join the fight.

"Don't even speak of it, Allie," one old woman told a ten-year-old. "You know you're not big enough to tote more than a carbine."

"But I'm a dead shot with it!" The little girl thrust her jaw out pugnaciously. "I can bring down a squirrel at a hundred yards!"

"So you can, and that'll suit us right fine when you're fourteen," said the old man sitting next to her. "Wait till you're old enough to carry a rifle, though."

"That'll be *forever*!"

Alea stared at them, shaken.

"What ails you, friend?" Grandma Em asked. "Never seen one so keen?"

"Not that young, no." Alea pushed back her chair and rose. "If you don't mind, Miz Farland, I'll go out and join the rifles."

"Yes, I think we should." Gar rose, too. "After all, you've given us hospitality."

Grandma Em frowned. "Can you shoot?"

"Of course." Alea didn't mention that she'd never used a gun that fired bullets, only raw bursts of energy.

The old woman considered the issue, frowning, then pronounced her judgment. " 'Tain't fitten for guests to take sides, and poor hospitality if we let you go into danger."

"We can't just sit here idle while people may be dying!" Gar objected.

Grandma Em smiled. "You sound like that eager little one there."

"I'm a bit older than ten," Alea said tartly.

Grandma Em relented. "Well, that's so. Go and watch, then, and maybe help with the wounded if the shooting moves past them. But don't let yourself get into the line of fire, you hear?"

"We hear," Alea said, "and we promise. Come on, Gar."

She rushed for the doorway; he was only a step behind her.

Grandma Em smiled after them, nodding her head slowly, and if the gleam in her eye was shrewd, who was there to notice?

As soon as they were out in the yard with people rushing past too quickly to listen, Alea said, "I'll scan the other boundaries. You sound out the main force of Belinkuns."

Gar nodded, his eyes losing focus. Alea turned away with a shudder; it seemed as though the man became a mindless body. Of course, she went into the same sort of trance herself, listening for the Belinkuns' thoughts, but that didn't matter—she didn't have to watch it.

There they were, a score of Belinkuns slipping through the northern field, bowing low so that the ears of maize above their heads would hide them. But Alea listened for other thoughts, other minds. She sensed the sharp wordless impulses of hungry creatures, the unvoiced delight of those who had found some food, but strongest and most clearly of all, the feelings of excitement and zeal from the humans who stole through the northwest woods, following the gully of the stream that made the land unfarmable, their thoughts keen with the hunter's delight, exultant with the anticipation of victory. She counted the different thought signatures, personalities as clearly different as their faces, then said to Gar, low-voiced, "They're in the northwest woods."

Gar's eyes refocused; he nodded. "What do we do about them, though?"

With distress, Alea realized that she had already felt the impulse to call to Martha and tell her where her enemy lay.

"Competition comes naturally to our species," Gar told her.

"Yes, but do I so quickly identify with one clan?"

Gar shrugged. "We've spent a few hours with them. They're real to us now, but we don't know the others at all."

"We're here to make peace," Alea said grimly, "not to help one clan wipe out the other."

Gar nodded. "Besides, they'd just pick a fight with the clan across the Belinkuns' boundary, and you'd have another feud going. Better if you go with the reserves and I go with Isaac's party, and we both try to scare off the others with as little bloodshed as possible."

Alea felt her back go up. "Why do I get the reserves?"

"Good question," Gar said. "You go with Isaac's party and I'll go with Martha's. Good hunting."

He strode away, leaving Alea looking after him, wondering if she had won a point or been manipulated.

Then she sighed, shrugged, and went off to join Isaac's force.

The Farlands were grinning and boastful as they set out.

" 'Bout time we got some action again!"

"You said it, Rilla! I been getting so rusty I can fairly hear my joints creak!"

"Ain't had nothing to shoot at that stood a chance of shooting back in way too long," one of the young men averred. "My aim's likely off by most of an inch now!"

"An inch!" a young woman hooted. "Ezra, if you can shoot within a foot of your mark today, I'll call it spring fever!"

But the farther they went from the house, the fewer the boasts became, until they crossed the fence into the pasture before the woods, and the whole force fell silent. Alea glanced from side to side and saw tense and glowering faces, jaw muscles bunched, eyes narrowing with remembered injuries.

Then they were in among the trees. Even in their thick-soled boots, the Farlands made almost no noise as they faded out of sight to either side with little more sound than the wind.

Alea swallowed hard and tried to imitate them, slipping from bush to bush, keeping a sharp eye open for twigs that might snap and give her away, but Isaac suddenly appeared beside her, whispering, "Best you stay here, ma'am. Anybody can tell where you are just from the noise."

Alea stared at him, then whispered back, "What noise?"

"Cloth against leaves, for one," Isaac answered, "and a dozen others too small to single out. Just wait for us here. We'll tell you when there's need of you."

Then he was gone and Alea sat on her heels, simmering. To vindicate herself, she opened her mind, tracing Isaac's progress from stump to trunk to bush—but she had to admit she would never have heard him with her ears.

Then she opened her mind forward and sensed the Belinkuns waiting in ambush.

Gar stayed well to the rear, but his height allowed him to keep Martha's white-flecked red hair, peeking from below the brown brim of her hat, in sight. As they neared the northeastern boundary, a low fieldstone wall, he could feel the Belinkuns tensing as they saw her, feel the keenness of their anticipation, knew that one or two were already leveling barrels and centering her in their sights—but he couldn't for the life of him see them, or even guess where they were hiding. The field had been mowed a few days before and was a long rise of stubble. True, a stream bed meandered through it and there were ditches to either side, but surely Martha and her troop were quick to see that.

Then a bird warbled and Martha sank to her knees, suddenly disappearing from view. So did her dozen clansfolk.

Gar blinked, astounded. If he hadn't been able to follow them by their thoughts, he wouldn't have known how they did it, but with telepathy, he realized that Martha had made the bird-cry herself, that it had been the signal, and that hearing it, everyone had found a hiding place, be it so little as a fold in the ground or a clump of weeds. Looking down from his seven-foot height, he could see them but only because he was behind them and knew where to look.

Then he realized that the only person left visible was himself—and that he was very visible indeed.

He threw himself to the ground as a rifle cracked in front of him. He heard the ball cut the air where he had been standing. A Farland rifle answered it, then two more, then three. The Belinkuns answered with a whole fusillade, but the bullets whizzed overhead, hurting no one, for everyone was down.

That wouldn't last. Gar could already hear both clans thinking that the only way they would be able to stop the others was by taking the risk of rising up long enough to spot an enemy and squeeze off a shot, then drop down again—but they also knew the risk, and knew that they might die. Memories reeled by at the association and Gar saw that every one of them had seen relatives killed in just such a fashion.

Nonetheless, their resolve hardened, each and every one, to take exactly that risk. To them, it was worth their lives to protect their loved ones from their villainous neighbors.

It wasn't worth it to Gar. He could see that the Belinkuns were just as good as the Farlands—no better, perhaps, struggling against their own human load of vices and weaknesses, but no worse, either. Gar couldn't see letting them die because of a centuries-old crime—but how could he stop them?

Distract them, of course.

They were all lying on the earth. What would they think if it began to move? Or if the sticks and leaves around them began to burn?

Too showy and too slow. So much for earth and fire. Gar decided on air and wood. He stared at the trunks, picking out the dead trees that were still standing, or fallen but caught by the branches of their neighbors. The smallest was a foot and a half thick, but they blurred as his attention focused on the air high above. He set up waves, like a cook stirring soup with a spoon, but stirring faster and faster.

One or two of the clansfolk looked up, startled, as the wind began to moan through the branches above. The sky had been clear when they came into the forest, and was still clear when leaves blew aside enough to show a patch of blue. Where was the breeze coming from?

The wind was whirling nicely now, making a gyre, a spinning funnel of air. Gar used it as a spear, hurling it downward. The narrow end plunged, tearing leaves off their stems and spinning them into itself. Gar could see it now, a green whorl that he used to strike one of the leaning trees, to tear it loose from its neighbor's fork . . .

The Belinkuns looked up, startled, hearing wood groan above.

Gar couldn't have that, couldn't have just one side distracted. He made the whirlwind bounce back up, then strike again, but much closer to him, strike with far more force than its size owned, strike at a hollow tree in the middle of the Farlands.

The Belinkuns shouted in alarm and dodged backward out of the way as the skeleton of a forty-foot oak slammed down in their midst. Half of them were in plain sight and no doubt would have fallen to the Farlands' guns—except that the Farlands were shouting in fear and anger as the hollow tree exploded in their midst. They ducked low as chunks of wood sprayed over their heads, then leaped to their feet and dashed away from the moaning, bobbing whirlwind—dashed until they remembered the human threat and turned, leveling their rifles at the first enemy they saw.

So much for wind and wood. Gar set his jaw and reached down into the ground, far below, feeling out the shape and form of the bedrock, finding the water deep below it and a fissure in the rock above. He widened the fissure just a little, molecules compacting against one another . . .

With a roar, the earth jolted just as the rifles blasted. Shots went wide; Farlands and Belinkuns fell, rifles flying from their hands. One or two scrambled to their knees and loosed a shot at the enemy, but the earth bucked again and their shots went wide. The clansfolk kept hold of their firearms, but fingers squeezed triggers by accident as they fell and stocks slammed into earth or wood, jarring the hammers into falling. The forest resounded with a fusillade of shots. Three people cried out with pain, one Belinkun and two Farlands wounded by stray shots, but none others.

For a moment, the forest lay quiet.

Then, howling, both clans shot to their feet and charged one another, not daring to take the time to reload lest their enemies catch them unarmed. Instead they swung their rifles like clubs, each long barrel suddenly serving as an iron quarterstaff.

Coming through the northwestern woods, the Belinkuns may have made noise enough, but now that they knew the Farlands were on their way, they went to ground so thoroughly that Alea knew she would never have seen them with her eyes. They waited crouched behind bushes and stumps and trunks with legs hardened against cramping by a lifetime's training, caressing their rifles, checking the priming now and again to make sure it was still dry and ready. The Farlands were searching for just such an ambush with eyes long trained to forest shadows, but what would happen if they failed to find the Belinkuns?

Come to that, what would happen if they did?

More to both points, how could Alea give away their positions without bloodshed?

The gunpowder, of course. None of them would kill any of the others if the powder refused to fire.

There was moisture in the air under the leaves—moisture from the evening that had condensed into dew and evaporated again with the sun, but was still held in the green gloom. She could gather that moisture into miniscule droplets, make it condense out into the fine gunpowder in the priming pans—all of the priming pans, Farland and Belinkun alike, condense into moisture more and more, until the powder became thick as paste—and she had to do it quickly, before any one of the clansfolk found any of the others. Moisture gathered on her forehead, too—fine drops of sweat raised by her efforts.

Somewhere off among the leaves, a trigger clicked and flint clashed into a pan. Someone howled at the discovery of treachery and an answering click sounded, an answering clash. Then the woods erupted with banshee howls as Farland saw Belinkun, howls that drowned out the clacking of flint in pan, useless clacking, shedding sparks into powder that was far too wet to fire.

Alea breathed a long, trembling sigh of relief.

Too soon, for people who carry flintlocks know well what to

do if the enemy falls upon them before they can reload. Roaring with anger, Belinkuns leaped upon Farlands swinging their rifles by the barrels, stocks smashing down at skulls. Shrilling rage, the Farlands met the swings with flintlocks held by stock and barrel, and in minutes the two forces were smashing furiously at one another in quarterstaff play with long rifles instead of staves.

Hiding behind her bush, Alea shuddered and consoled herself with the thought that quarterstaves, even ones shod with iron, were far less lethal than rifles.

Then she heard Gar's voice inside her head. *I made their shots go wide, but they're charging out to club one another to death.*

Alea almost went limp with relief—she wasn't alone. *Mine, too. How can we stop them?*

We need a vantage point first. Find a tall tree and persuade a bird to do your looking for you. To illustrate, Gar showed her the world from a bird's-eye view. The bird in question was perched on a lower limb of a pine, to judge from the needles that framed the scene, and had an excellent view of the ragged lines of flailing fighters.

It was a good technique. Alea had never tried it before, but it only took a few seconds to find a crow with the right viewpoint and tap into its bird brain. It huddled against the trunk, frightened by the loud noises, but stayed frozen in place, afraid to attract attention, watching the fighters for any sign that they might decide to come its way.

Then, before either of them could do anything to stop the fighting, a wave of dizziness rocked her.

5

It passed, and her lips thinned in anger, but she had to admit it worked beautifully. The clansfolk were swinging wildly and connecting with nothing. The dizziness didn't seem to have passed for them; woodsfolk who had been silent minutes before went crashing through the underbrush calling for their enemies to stand still, which of course they didn't; they too plunged about, flailing with their rifles and shouting in anger.

Alea wanted to ask Gar something, but she was too confused to remember what. She reached out for his mind but found only disorientation there, too. In a panic, she could only think to go to him—why, she couldn't say, she only knew that it was important. She stood up and staggered away, following the feel of his thoughts, swirling though they might be. She blundered into thorns and even splashed through a brook before she saw it was there, but somehow recognized a bog in time to go around it. Tree trunks reeled past her; she knew what they were, but didn't understand why they kept trying to get into her way. All the while, she felt Gar's thoughts coming nearer, though, and that was all that mattered.

The dizzy spell began to recede as he came in sight. Relief

made her want to clutch at him, but made her indignant, too, so by the time she came to him, she only said, "Why didn't you warn me you were going to do that?"

Gar only blinked at her, bemused. "You mean it wasn't your doing?"

Alea felt a chill spread through her vitals. "I wouldn't know how."

Gar gazed off into space, frowning in thought. "I suppose I could figure out a way, but I didn't." He turned back to her, brow furrowed. "But if we didn't—who did?"

Alea stared up at him, nonplussed. Then she reached out for the thoughts of the clansfolk. Gar realized what she was doing and searched, too.

"Whatever did it, it seems to have worked wonderfully. The Belinkuns and the Farlands are all going home, and no one died."

"A few casualties, though," Gar said. "We'll have to make sure Joram doesn't lose that leg."

"Sukey's arm should heal, though." Alea frowned. "I'll have to make sure it's bound." She turned toward the Farlands' thoughts. "We'd better join them—we have work to do."

"Yes, and we'll have to find some way to reach the Belinkuns." Gar fell in beside her.

"Still," Alea said, "I wonder what could have caused that disorientation."

"It might have been the earthquake," Gar conjectured.

Alea stared at him, then swung around to confront him. "What earthquake?"

"A small localized one," Gar hedged. "It only hit where Martha's band was fighting. Made all the shots go wide, though."

"How convenient," Alea said drily. "Tell me—how do you cause an earthquake?"

They wended homeward, discussing ways and means of neutralizing clan fights, forgetting about their sudden confusion for the time being.

Deep in the forest, Evanescent's cat-smile widened.

• • •

Isaac's band hadn't gone very far from the wood; they were milling about, discussing something with more emotion than sense. Isaac looked up, saw her coming and cried, "There you are! Thank Heaven! We couldn't find you and thought the Belinkuns had captured you."

"I'm sorry to worry you." Alea joined them. "You told me to stay well back, so I climbed a tree. I thought I should wait until the Belinkuns were gone before I came down."

"That you should, but we were worried nonetheless." Isaac turned to his band. "No need to follow the Belinkuns now. They'll not come too quickly to our borders again. Home we go."

With a shock, Alea realized they'd been arguing about whether or not to follow the Belinkuns, thinking they had kidnapped her. No wonder they hadn't gone very far.

"A moment," Alea said, and went over to the litter where Joram lay, jaw clenched, a length of bloodstained cloth tied about his thigh. With her thoughts, she reached inside the wound to explore, then asked, "Has he been tended?"

"All that we can do in the field," one of the women answered, "a poultice and a bandage. Back at the house, we'll have that bullet out with the long forceps and cauterize the wound."

Alea nodded, but she didn't like the sound of such primitive treatment. As they walked back toward the house, part of her mind was knitting muscle fibers inside Joram's wound, pushing the bullet closer and closer to the surface. By the time they took the bandage off, it should be only an inch deep.

The rest of her mind, though, was engaged in conversation. Walking beside the litter, she fell back to the woman who had spoken of the bandage. "I'm Alea."

"Don't I know it!" the other answered. "I'm Susanah."

"It must gall you to heal folk only to have them go out and argue with bullets again."

Susanah grimaced and answered low, "You wonder why you do it sometimes. Of course, there's delight when they recover, but there's dismay when next they march out—not that there's much choice."

"Wouldn't it be nice if there were," Alea said with a sigh.

"Wouldn't it just," Susanah said grimly. "At least Joram's the only one hurt bad in our band today, and no one died." She frowned. "Wonder why the powder failed?"

"Maybe there's a god of gunpowder," Alea quipped, "and he didn't like your fighting today."

Susanah looked up, staring. "You don't really think so, do you?"

Alea didn't, actually, but she felt a ghost of inspiration and followed up the thought. She shrugged her shoulders and said the vaguest thing she could. "Who knows about gods?"

Susanah looked away, muttering, "I always thought they were just stories, never real. Everyone does."

But Alea read in her a deep, almost desperate desire for something to believe in, and chose her words carefully. "You never can tell. There's no proof the gods exist, but there's no proof they don't, either."

"Grandma Em says you don't have to talk about gods to explain how everything started," Susanah answered, "that the Cosmic Egg hatched, and everything grew out of it as chicks grow into hens."

"It seems hard to believe," Alea said, "but there's a lot we don't understand."

"A great lot," Susanah muttered.

"Still, just because you can explain the world without the gods—well, that's not proving they don't exist, is it?"

Susanah turned to frown at her. "How's that?"

"We can prove that the world exists without me," Alea said. "In fact, up until yesterday you didn't even know I was alive. But that didn't prove I wasn't, did it?"

Susanah turned away, glowering.

"Gunpowder, now," Alea went on. "That's something men invented. There wouldn't be a god for it."

"Well, no," Susanah said, "but Morrigan, she's the goddess of war. Gunpowder would be hers, wouldn't it?"

"I suppose," Alea said, "but I think she'd be happy with fighting, not wanting to stop it."

"Not if we did it wrong," Susanah said. "Besides, there's oak and ash and rowan in that forest. They were sacred to the old gods, weren't they?"

"I—I really don't know," Alea stammered. Then inspiration struck again. "You'd have to ask a Druid."

"If there are any left," Susanah said with a sour smile.

Alea moved about among the clansfolk, chatting with one, listening to several others, and was amazed at what she heard. Only a few of the young ones were really eager for another battle, and Alea wondered if they would have been so fiery if they had been hit by a bullet. She looked into some of their minds and saw that they had been, and they now burned for revenge.

That same vengeful fire smoldered in several of the older ones too, for they'd seen loved ones killed in battle. One of the older men lectured a handful of his juniors. "There's no choice, you know, no way to deal with Belinkuns except by rifle. They're snakes, they'll turn on you as soon as you try to make peace. They'll bite the hand of friendship, for they'll take it as a sign of weakness."

But to Alea, his words rang hollow, for deep within him, beneath the layers of bitterness and hatred, she read a longing for a world in which neighbors could be friends.

The two bands met at the house. Old folk and children embraced sons, daughters, and parents with cries of delight. Susanah was amazed how shallow Joram's wound was, and Alea managed to catch Gar alone outside when they went to wash their hands in the trough.

"For a culture based on war," she said, "there are a surprising number of people here who don't want to fight."

"I know what you mean," he said. "I talked with a few on the way home and listened to a few more . . ."

"What they said, or what they didn't say?"

"Yes. No one is actually willing to come right out and say they want the feud to stop—they're afraid of their relatives thinking them cowards or, worse, even traitors."

"So the feud goes on because all the people who want it to stop don't dare speak up," Alea said grimly.

"It seems so. Everyone over the age of thirty wants to stop the feud, even the ones who talk tough, but no one can figure out how to do it."

"I found a few who weren't willing to let it go," Alea said slowly. "They're too bitter about friends and loved ones killed in the fighting—or absolutely convinced there's no way the Belinkuns would ever honor a treaty."

"That's sad to hear," Gar said with a grimace.

"I do have to say they're the bravest fighters I've ever seen," Alea said slowly.

Gar heard what she didn't say—that the clansfolk were braver than her own people, who had fought giants and dwarves out of sheer bigotry. It took little enough courage to fight those who were smaller than yourself, and not much more to fight giants when you outnumbered them so thoroughly. "They aren't all as brave as they seem, but they don't let their fear show; they've been raised that way."

"You mean some of them really are afraid of the fighting?" Alea asked.

"When they've seen fathers and aunts die in combat, yes. There are more of them who are simply disgusted with the pointlessness of it."

"Fear, disgust, outrage—and the list goes on," Alea mused. "How many don't want war?"

"Most of them, judging by what I hear," Gar said. "The women are sick of seeing husbands, sons, and lovers die. Even the ones who burn for revenge are disgusted with the carnage."

"And the men have stopped seeing the point of it," Alea said. "When they've been fighting half their lives, they begin to ask why, and what happened to their ancestors stops seeming important. The past is dead."

"But the living become vital," Gar said, "as they should."

A strident clanging rolled out through the evening air. Looking up, they saw one of the clansfolk running an iron rod around the inside of a metal triangle hung from a pole.

"I wondered what that was for," Alea said.

"Dinner call," Gar interpreted, "and a celebration of life after nearing death. Let's join them."

"Let's," Alea agreed. "What do you suppose confused us all, anyway?"

They left the next morning, with anxious well-wishing from the clansfolk. As they hiked out of earshot, Alea said, "That was very informative, but how much can we learn going from farmstead to farmstead this way?"

Gar looked down at her with barely concealed concern. "You're not thinking of going off on your own, are you?"

"Why not?" she asked, bristling. "I can take care of myself!"

"I don't doubt that," Gar said quickly, "but two are always safer than one."

"Oh, so you don't think I can cope with whatever comes along?"

"No, no! There's scarcely anything that could hurt you, with the skills you've learned."

"Then what are you worried about?" Alea demanded.

" 'Scarcely' could happen entirely too often," Gar explained.

"What's the matter?" Alea jibed. "Don't you trust your own teaching?"

"Now that you mention it," Gar said, "no."

"Then trust my learning!" Alea snapped. "I can read other people's thoughts now, at least well enough to find out if anyone with a rifle is lurking in the underbrush—and if they try attacking me with a knife or a stick, I can counter them with my staff."

"How many is 'them'?" Gar asked with a jaundiced eye.

"I'm up to three at once, you've said so yourself!"

"Unless they know tricks you don't."

"Which means their knowing tricks *you* don't! Or have you been holding out on me?"

"You've been making excellent progress . . ."

"So you *haven't* been telling me everything!"

"Well, I can't teach you all at once," Gar protested. "It takes years."

"It's *been* years!"

"Only two of them. Mind you, you're still able to cope with nine out of ten dangers you're apt to meet . . ."

"Then what are you worried about?"

"Number ten."

Alea felt a warm glow, hearing that he was worried about her. It added heat to her arguments. "You want me to be safe? I'll pose as a peddler! These people ought to honor traders—they're so starved for things they can't grow or make themselves! You should outfit yourself as a packman, too!"

"Good idea." Gar nodded.

Alea stared at him, stunned.

"It would give you a chance to hide a few hand grenades and a blaster among your trade goods," Gar explained.

That brought Alea out of her stupor. "We want less mayhem on this planet, not more! Show these people a grenade and they'll start cobbling them up themselves!"

"Well, all right, but they couldn't make blasters . . ."

"So you want them to discover research? Aren't there better ways to motivate them?"

It went on for a while longer, and all in all, she found it a highly satisfying argument. When Gar called up to Herkimer to drop two packs of trade goods during the night, though, that made her victory seem too easy. Alea developed a suspicion that Gar had been enjoying their verbal sparring as much as she had—either enjoying it or suffering from a vastly misplaced sense of chivalry. She had heard him argue much more strongly than that. As they settled down for the night, she reflected smugly that he definitely did care about her, even if it wasn't the passionate regard she craved.

She went stiff at the thought, staring unseeing at the night around them. What was she thinking? Passion? She certainly didn't want that!

They were on the road again as the sun rose and separated at the first fork.

"Be careful, now," Gar said anxiously.

"You be careful, too," Alea retorted, then turned back to him, frowning. "Wait a minute! All through this, you haven't said a word about your own safety!"

"Well, of course not."

"Oh, you're sure of being able to handle a small army all by yourself, are you?" Alea's eyes blazed.

"It's not that," Gar protested. "It's just that if *I* get hurt, it doesn't matter."

Alea stared at him, frozen for a second. Then she threw her arms around him and pressed her cheek against his chest. "It matters to me. It matters most horribly to me! Make sure you listen for thoughts on the road and duck away from them before they can hurt you!" She tilted her face up, gave him a quick kiss on the cheek, said, "Take care of yourself!" and turned to stalk away down the left-hand road, face flaming.

Gar stared at the back of her head, at the rich chestnut fall of her hair beneath the broad-brimmed hat, and pressed a hand to his cheek, bemused. When she had gone out of sight, he turned slowly away and started down the right-hand fork.

He had gone perhaps a hundred yards before he heard the double click of a rifle being cocked.

Gar dove off the road and into the underbrush as the gun blasted.

6

Gar heard the ball smack into a tree trunk, heard two other rifles crack, one from ahead, one from the far side of the road and to the rear. He turned, gathering himself and readying his staff even as his mind searched for his attackers.

There they were, reloading their rifles, thoughts hot with avarice and rank with resentment and rage. Gar crouched in the underbrush, waiting, silent. Finally a voice from ahead called, "He's dead, Lem."

"He'd better be, with you calling out like a banshee," Lem answered in a furious whisper. Gar tracked the voice—the man to the left, the one who had shot first.

"He's out cold, at least," the voice from behind answered.

"Or playing possum," Lem answered. "What's got into you, Farrell? You used to know better than to sound off!"

"Aw, he can't hurt us," the first voice said. "Didn't have no rifle, anyways—and no clan; he's just a trader."

"Then every clan would be out to avenge him! Okay, Zeke, we'll go look, but you better hope it's out cold, and not dead, if you don't want the Farlands teaming up with the Gillicutties and the Orkneys to clean us out of these woods!"

"We'll be right beside you, loaded and cocked," Zeke assured him. "What's he going to do when he's looking down three gun barrels, hey?"

It was a good question, Gar decided. As a precaution, he focused his thoughts into gathering moisture into the pans of the flintlocks, saturating the priming powder into sludge. It wouldn't go off even if one of them did manage to squeeze a trigger, but Gar didn't intend to give them the chance.

Lem came close first, but stopped six feet short of the underbrush to wait for his friends to come up. With a man of normal height that might have been enough, but Gar shot out of the brambles staff first, extending his seven feet of length into ten.

The butt caught Lem in the belly and he folded, mouth gaping in pain as the rifle dropped from his fingers.

Farrell shouted in anger and came running, but Lem called, "Stay back!" Gar heard his hammer click in the pan, then his curse at the gun's refusing to fire.

Farrell had paused, but now he charged in again, rifle leveled for a point-blank shot. Gar swung his staff, knocking it away. The useless hammer clicked and Gar swung the end of the staff to crack against Farrell's head.

Zeke shouted in anger. Gar whirled to see him charging in, face red and distorted with rage, swinging his rifle by the barrel, stock arcing down at Gar where he still crouched by the roadside.

He waited for the moment, then shot to his feet, and the rifle butt cracked against Gar's staff. Zeke backed away, round-eyed, staring up at the giant who seemed to have sprouted from the earth.

But Lem had caught enough breath to get back in the fight. He launched himself at Gar's shins, his body a wrecking ball.

Gar shouted with anger as he fell. Zeke yelped with relief and charged back in, rifle swinging, even as Lem rolled up to his feet and swung his rifle barrel in a short vicious arc.

It caught Gar across the shoulders and striped his back with pain, but only added its force to his momentum as he turned the fall into a dive, the dive into a somersault, and shot to his feet right under Zeke's nose, fist swinging in an uppercut. He pulled his punch and the fist only caught the man's chin. Zeke staggered back, raising his rifle to guard and Gar twisted it from his hands.

He swung to face Lem with a rifle in one hand and a staff in the other, both raised to swing. "Put it down, Lem, or I'll put it down for you."

The woodsman froze, glaring in baffled anger. Then he took refuge in a face-saver. "How'd you know my name?"

"Heard you talking to one another, of course," Gar said. "Put down the rifle."

Lem measured his own five-and-a-half-feet against Gar's height and muscle, then spat a curse and laid down his rifle.

"Go see how badly Farrell's hurt," Gar directed, "then bring him back here—without his rifle." He stepped back and pivoted so that he could see both men. "Come on over, Zeke. I want your rifle, too."

"The hell you say!"

"I'll take it from you awake or out cold, just as you choose," Gar said evenly. "It would be easier for you if I didn't have to knock you on the head."

Zeke gave Lem an uncertain glance. The leader's mouth twisted with chagrin, but he gave a brief nod. Zeke stepped forward, reversing the weapon to offer it to Gar stock first.

Gar took it and said, "Help Lem see to Farrell. I tried not to hit him too hard, but you never know."

The hint of mercy seemed to unnerve them more than his anger had. Lem turned and waded into the brush after Farrell, Zeke close behind. Gar took both guns by the barrels in one hand, held his staff ready in the other, and followed them closely.

Farrell was propped up on one elbow, head in one hand.

Lem's voice softened as he knelt. "Bad as that, ol' buddy?"

"Hard fist." Farrell tried to sound disgusted, but it came out as a croak.

"It wasn't no fist, it was the end of his stick," Lem said, as though a staff against a rifle were unfair odds.

"I'll be okay." Farrell reached up. "Just help me stand."

Lem beckoned Zeke, who stepped around and took Farrell's other arm.

"I don't need that much help," Farrell protested, but he leaned on both of them as they drew him to his feet.

"Are both his pupils the same size?" Gar asked.

"Pupils?" Lem turned to frown. "He ain't no schoolmarm!"

"The little black circles in his eyes." Gar strove for patience. "Are they both the same size?"

Lem glared hatred at him, but turned to look.

Now that Gar could see them up close, his victory ceased to impress him. All three men were gaunt with hunger and scabbed with the sores of vitamin deficiencies—all in all, a pretty scruffy crew. Of course, they'd had rifles, but he had put those out of action at the outset. Feeling a little guilty, he said, "Lousy timing—you ambushed me just as I was thinking of stopping to eat." He swung his pack off his shoulder, unstrapped it one-handed, and took out a loaf and a wedge of cheese.

All three men stared at the food, transfixed. Lem asked hoarsely, "You planning to just eat that while we watch?"

"Why, would you like some?" Gar held out the loaf.

Lem grabbed the bread, tore off a chunk for himself, then two more for his friends and reluctantly handed it back.

"It's pretty simple fare," Gar said, "but if one of you will build a fire and another fetch water, we can stew some salt beef till it's soft enough to chew."

"Reckon we can do that," Lem conceded. "Got a bucket?"

Gar handed him the folding canvas pail.

Lem took it and turned away. "You boys build the man a fire, now."

Zeke did, with the efficiency of long practice, piling tinder and arranging sticks in a cone over it. " 'Course, if I had my rifle, I could snap a spark in there right quick. 'Thout it, though, I'll have to rub two sticks."

"Stand back," Gar said.

The two men retreated. Gar knelt with one eye on them and one on the fire, then cocked one of the unloaded rifles, held it on its side, and pulled the trigger. There was no report, of course, but the flint struck sparks from the pan. They fell into the tinder, and Gar struck twice more, then stepped back. Zeke knelt again and breathed carefully on the sparks until flames blossomed. By the time Lem came back with the dripping bucket, they had a merry campfire burning.

They sat on their heels around the flames, munching bread and cheese while the aroma of stewing beef spread through the air. Gar let his gaze roam around the clearing and said, "It's better out here—away from the smells and noise of the towns. Too many people."

"Wouldn't know about towns," Zeke grumbled.

"Even the farms," Gar qualified. "Barnyard smells, fifty people at one meal all in the same hall—too many for the space, at least."

"Too many people who don't like to hear the truth," Lem said with disgust.

"Not many who do," Gar said, his interest piqued. "The townsfolk believe that a naked Truth lives in the bottom of each village well."

"Couldn't," Farrell said. "There'd be too much of it in the water, and the folks couldn't stomach that."

"Naked?" Zeke's eyes glinted. "What would happen if she came out?"

"A man named Hans Sachs wrote about that once," Gar said. "Truth told a man and a woman how tormented and lonely she was, and they felt sorry for her and embraced her—until she started telling them each the truth about themselves."

Lem actually laughed—a hard and brittle sound, but a laugh. "What'd the man and woman do then?"

"Chased her back into the well," Gar said.

"Figures," Farrell snorted.

Lem nodded. "I spoke the truth once."

"Really." Gar tried to keep from pouncing on it. "What happened?"

"They chased *me* away for it," Lem said bitterly, "my own kith and kin!"

Farrell nodded. "I wasn't that dumb, but almost. Started talking as how what happened three hundred years ago shouldn't matter now."

"They chased you away, too?" Gar asked.

"Not until three or four cousins started allowing as how I was making sense." Farrell turned and spat. "Grandpa said I was takin' the starch out of the whole clan, and if we did that, them Elroys would just roll right over us. The great aunts agreed with him, so they kicked me out to warn the others."

"You have the same story?" Gar asked Zeke.

The woodsman flushed and looked away.

"No, he was different," Lem said. "Couldn't take his eyes off his cousin's wife, and couldn't talk to her without sounding sweet."

Gar frowned. "But he didn't *do* anything."

"No, but you can't have that kind of thing," Lem said. "Sooner or later cousins will start fighting if there's a woman between 'em—and you need to be fighting the enemy clan, not your own."

"Didn't do nothin' at all," Zeke grunted. "Not like Orville, not atall."

The other two men suddenly became fascinated by the sight of the broth bubbling in the kettle.

"What did Orville do?" Gar asked.

"Coward talk," Lem said.

"Can't say why." Farrell frowned, puzzled. "He's a brave man, the kind to go up against a bear with nothing but a knife."

"Yeah, but he'd already shot his rifle, and that didn't stop the boar-bear," Zeke objected. "Five more men shot it, too, before it reached him."

"But he held his ground," Farrell objected.

"Swung aside at the last minute," Lem reminded him.

"Yeah, but that's just good fighting," Farrell countered. "He still stood with that knife up, waiting to see if the bear turned on him."

"It didn't?" Gar guessed.

"No, it stumbled on and lay dead," Farrell told him. "Don't change how brave he was, though."

"So what kind of 'coward talk' did this brave man make?" Gar asked.

The men glanced at one another, clearly unwilling to talk about it even now. At last Lem said, "That there weren't no point to people getting killed when they didn't have to—that folks don't *have* to fight, and surely not to the death."

"Coward talk, all right." Zeke nodded with conviction. "So he's out here with the rest of us now, and it's kill or be killed for sure."

"Only if the clans get together to clean us out," Lem demurred.

"Yeah, or unless another band tries to take our food," Zeke shot back.

Farrell nodded. "Least that makes sense—killing to get food for starving folks."

"Not like killing 'cause one great-great-fifty-times-great grandpa shot another." Lem stood up. "Enough talk. Time to hike home if we want to get there before dark." He looked down at Gar. "Come if you want, stranger. The roof might be only straw, but it's better than sleeping out in the open."

"It does feel like rain," Gar admitted. "Do you always invite the people you ambush home?"

"Sure—why not?" Lem grinned. "Once we've got their food and their goods, leastways. They don't usually accept, though."

Gar shrugged. "Why not? I'm a trader, and your people

might have furs to swap for needles." He stood and started kicking dirt over the fire.

The outlaws began to relax on the way home, becoming downright talkative. Gar only had to toss in the occasional question to steer the conversation toward the outlaw life and the reasons for taking it up; the men were quick enough to argue the merits of their comrades' cases. When Lem claimed that the youngest of their number, a teenager named Kerlew, had been outcast for being a weakling and just downright strange, Farrell objected.

"Kerlew ain't no weakling," he said. "He's made it through three winters with nothing worse than a head cold, and he's always brought in his share of squirrel meat."

"Makes good gunpowder, too," Zeke observed.

Lem grinned at Gar. "You notice they don't try to say he isn't strange."

"Well, he does get that faraway look in his eye a lot," Zeke admitted.

"And he talks about the gods like he really believes in 'em." Farrell shook his head in despair.

"His clan cast him out for no more than that?" Gar asked in disbelief.

"He likely would have run away on his own, sooner or later," Zeke opined. "They made fun of him so much, it's a wonder he stayed till he was eighteen."

"Thought he had nothing to lose," Lem explained to Gar, "so he started preaching peace—and by oak, ash, and thorn, that boy can preach!"

"But his clan declared him a coward and cast him out?" Gar asked.

"A coward and a traitor, for making the Murrays doubt themselves and their cause," Lem said, bitter again. "Thought he weakened their backbones."

"Now he stiffens ours," Farrell said. "If you don't think the outlaw life is the right life, stranger, you just ask young Kerlew, and you'll be dazed by his answer."

"You think this life is right and good?" Gar asked in amazement.

" 'Course we do." Lem looked him straight in the eye. "We don't have to kill no one for no good reason, stranger—or for the sake of a quarrel hundreds of years gone, which amounts to the same thing."

"We'll kill if another band tries to kill us," Farrell said, "but I'll tell you, none of us can remember the last time that happened."

" 'Course, you don't live to be all that old, with only thin walls to keep out the cold, and with bears and wolves against you," Lem pointed out. "But the word gets passed down. Eighty years since one band tried to kill off another for their food, that's what we figure."

"That's very good," Gar said. "I should think hunger would drive you to it more often than that."

"It might, if the clans didn't club together to wipe us out every so often," Zeke said bitterly.

"When you tell it that way, I'm surprised there's anyone who doesn't join you in the forest," Gar said.

Lem eyed him askance. "You know what 'outlaw' means, stranger?"

"Happens that I do," Gar said. "It means that you broke the law, put yourself outside it, so you lose its protection. Anyone can kill you for any reason, and your clan won't avenge you."

Lem nodded. "So anybody from any clan can beat us up or steal from us or kill us off—if they're fool enough to come into the deep woods, where every tree trunk might have a sharpshooter ready to kill *them*."

"But it means no healing if you're sick, and none of the goods you can make on a homestead," Farrell pointed out.

Gar nodded slowly. "Good reasons to stay within the law, even if you don't really agree with it. You'd have to be awfully sick of fighting to stand up and walk out. Do all the clans have those laws?"

"There's stories about clans who didn't, but they died off," Farrell said offhandedly.

Gar felt a chill. He wondered if the tales had been true, and talk against war really did make a clan weak—or if they were simply stories made up to frighten clansfolk into doing as they were told.

"You do get sick and tired of the fighting if you live long enough," Zeke allowed, " 'specially if you get to know somebody from the other clan and find out how much they're like you."

"And there's always some who do," Lem sighed, "and who fall in love."

Gar felt the chill again. "You sound as if you know what you're talking about."

"We've got two in our band right now," Lem said, "and it's a miracle they're still in love, after the way they starved and just barely managed till we found them."

"Allie is a Rork," Farrell said, "and Billy is a Gonigle. Hard for young folk not to meet each other, when the same stream flows through both their farms."

"But if their clans didn't live next to each other, they wouldn't be fighting?"

"Seems to be the way of it," Lem sighed.

"Good fences make good neighbors," Farrell added, "but it seems the ancestors didn't believe that."

"So we've been learning it the hard way ever since," Lem said sourly.

Gar steered the conversation back to crime. "Didn't they try to hide the fact that they were in love?"

"Oh, they tried," Lem said, "but good luck keeping anything secret from your clan. You're going to go sneaking off far too often, and sooner or later there'll be a pair of eyes to watch you go."

"And a pair of silent feet to follow you," Farrell added.

"Somebody got curious, and trailed one of them?" Gar asked.

"One of the Rork girls, as Allie tells it," Lem said, "a little one. You know how the tads are about spying on the big ones when folks come a' courting. Well, the child followed Allie . . ."

"Fun game," Zeke said generously.

"Yeah, tracking without being spotted," Lem agreed. "The tad was too good at it, though, and Allie didn't suspect a thing, though I'm sure she must have been wary . . ."

"When she was on her way to meet Billy?" Farrell asked. "She might have missed a few twigs breaking."

"No doubt," Lem agreed. "But the tad saw her meet Billy, saw her kiss him, and ran straight home, bursting with the news."

"Poor kid probably didn't think she'd get Allie in trouble for anything more than kissing," Zeke sighed.

"Likely not. But she told, all bright-eyed and bursting with the excitement of it, and her grandma sent out a dozen men to bring the lovers in."

"That time, she did hear something," Farrell said.

"She says she heard a jaybird calling at night," Lem went on, "and knew right away what was coming, so she sent Billy running right quick."

"Musta been someone in the clan who cared about her," Zeke said. "Only a fool would give a jay call at night."

Lem nodded. "Next thing she heard was gunshots."

Gar stared. "And they're both still alive to tell of it?"

"You ever try hitting a target at night, when it's twisting and turning 'mongst moon shadows?" Farrell asked.

"I have, yes." Gar didn't think it necessary to tell them that the weapon had been a crossbow. "I see your point."

"So her clan gathered to judge, and cast her out," Lem said. "But the tad felt bad about it and went to tell Billy—he was hanging around down by the creek hoping to see her again."

"Her grandma sent a truce party to tell the Gonigles first, though," Farrell said, "and they sat in judgment and cast out Billy."

"Good thing, too," Farrell agreed. "If they hadn't, he'd have upped and run away to find Allie, and his kinfolk would have come after to shoot him for treachery."

Gar stared, aghast. "There's no sense in that."

Lem shrugged. "There's no sense in feuding either, stranger, but try and stop it."

"We did," said Farrell, "most of the folks in our band, one way or another."

Gar frowned. "Wouldn't both clans have hunted them down for outlawry?"

"Just for the hell of it, you mean?" Lem nodded. "There's always some like that. Too much killing, and most folks grow to hate it, but some grow to like it. That's why they lit out."

"Strangers would hate them less than their own clans," Farrell observed. "No reason to think them traitors."

"Oh." Gar thought that over. "So this all happened far away?"

"A month's travel," Lem said. "Probably would have gone farther, if they hadn't come across a band that welcomed them."

"We did." Farrell nodded. "They're good kids."

"Our kind," Zeke agreed.

Gar appreciated the irony of it—that the ones who turned vicious were still welcomed in their own clans, as long as they didn't torment their own, whereas the ones who sickened of the slaughter and took a stand against it, were outlawed. "What if someone kills a person in his own clan?"

"Oh, he'll be killed in his own turn," Lem answered, "so those who do usually light out before they can be caught."

"There are vicious outlaws too, then?"

"Some," Farrell said, his voice hard. "When we find 'em, we kill 'em, too."

Gar frowned. "That seems harsh."

"How do you think we find out, stranger?" Lem challenged. "They try to hurt someone in the band, that's how! It comes down to kill or be killed, really."

"You could cast them . . . no, I see the point. An outcast from the outcasts is likely to haunt the woods looking for folk out on their own, waiting for a chance for revenge."

"We never go out alone," Lem said, "but accidents happen."

Gar could imagine it, one of the outlaws thinking they would be safe just this once, going a hundred yards from the camp for a bucket of water from the stream. "What happens if someone steals?"

"From another clan?" Zeke grinned. "He's a hero!"

"No, from his own clan."

"Oh! Well, if they find it out, he's outlawed."

" 'Course, it's been known for one clan member to accuse another, and talk a third into lying about it before the family council," Farrell said judiciously, "but it doesn't happen often."

"Why not?" Gar asked, afraid of the answer.

"Why, because the liar's outlawed, too." Farrell looked up at Gar. "Mind you, nobody minds the odd lie here and there, in the daily round—you have to be wary and take your chances. But before the council, now, when someone else's doom is hanging—well, that's something else."

"I can see that it would be." So they outlawed treachery in even the slightest form, and cowardice, murder, theft, and false witness—but only within the clan. "I suppose if a clansman falls in love with a cousin's wife and she falls in love with him, they just run away and find an outlaw band to join?"

"If they can," Lem said, with flat cynicism.

"More likely the clan will hunt them down and bring them back for trial," Farrell said.

"*Then* they'll cast 'em out," Zeke finished.

"Has to be done the right way, eh? How about if a single man falls in love with his cousin, and gets her pregnant?"

"That's punishable by marriage," Zeke said, grinning, "as long as the cousin isn't too close—by blood, anyway."

"Second cousins are okay," Lem said, "but it's better to marry into the next county."

"Oh." Gar raised his eyebrows. "You get together with other clans?"

"Sure," Farrell said with a sardonic smile. "The clans who share a boundary with you, you'll fight to the death, but the one ten miles away, well now, they'll be your friends."

"Especially if they live right next to your neighbors, but on the other side," Lem explained. " 'Course, you have to go to the parties all together, but folks don't generally ambush then."

An unwritten law, Gar guessed, without which every clan would spend its whole life cooped up on the same few acres and die off from inbreeding.

It made sense, in its way. All of the "crimes" the three outlaws had spoken of weakened the unity of the clan and its ability to fight without mercy. Apparently, now and then, enough outlaws survived to form a band such as the one toward which they were going. He suspected that over a few generations the band would become a clan in its own right.

He wondered how long it took the new band to start a feud of its own and to begin outlawing its lawbreakers.

All at once the trees opened out on either side into a clearing perhaps a hundred yards across. Toward its center stood a ring of stoutly built, thatch-roofed log cottages. Pigs rooted about in the grass circle at the center, and children ran about with men and women watching them as they worked at household chores.

Gar stared. Apparently the band had been going longer than he had thought. "This is your home camp?"

"That it is, stranger, and we'll thank you to shuck your pack and put up your hands." Lem nodded toward the cottages, grinning. "Maybe you can fight three rifles, but how about a dozen?"

More than that—a score of outlaws had seen them, and were coming toward them with their rifles leveled.

7

G ar had to decide, and decide instantly. Should he over-
awe the outlaws with displays that they would call magic,
and take the chance that they would think him a witch? Or use
his mental powers in such a way that they wouldn't know how
he had won?

Neither. One man just couldn't win against twelve, no matter
how good a fighter he was. Gar called out, "Whoever thinks to
lead this band, let him prove it against me, hand to hand!"

The outlaws stopped, staring in consternation, then turned
to one another in furious debate.

Lem grinned. "Think you're fit to lead us, stranger? Just kill
off our chief and call yourself boss? That's not our way."

"I wasn't thinking of taking the title," Gar said evenly, "or
the job. I only want the man to prove he deserves it, that's all."

"You just might get your chance." Lem watched, grinning
with anticipation. So did Farrell, and Zeke chuckled.

Gar frowned. What was he missing?

Then a woman stepped forward, handing her rifle to the
man beside her and taking off her hat and jacket. "I'm Rowena,
stranger, and I'm the chosen chief of this band."

Gar stared. Admittedly, she was a big woman, both tall and stocky, her body having thickened with age. Gray streaked the long black hair that was tied in a club at the base of her neck. Surely, though, she didn't really think she stood a chance against a man twenty years younger than she—twenty years younger, a foot and half taller, and half again as heavy!

"We choose our leader by wisdom, not fighting," Lem explained. "You want to fight her hand to hand, you fight us all."

Gar stared at Rowena, digesting that for a minute. Then he nodded, shrugging out of his pack and taking off his hat. "That's better odds than fighting twelve rifles. Hand to hand it is, outlaws, twelve to one or not!"

The outlaws stared, taken aback by his boldness.

"You can't beat a hundred and more, stranger," Rowena said. "Don't be a fool."

Gar grinned, lifting his fists. "This isn't about wisdom."

Rowena's face darkened even more. "You'd be wiser to yield your pack and go your way. I've no wish to have your blood on my conscience."

"I told you she was wise," Lem said, then called to Rowena, "He seems to be a good one, though he's not willing to pay the toll."

"Toll, is it?" Gar asked. "All I own? Nothing left to sell or trade?"

Lem shrugged. "You can always start over."

"It's worth a fight to keep it."

"Have it as you will," Rowena said in disgust. "Take him, people."

The outlaws shouted and waded in, Rowena foremost. She was the first to swing at Gar, and he took the blow on his shoulder, rolling with the punch, not even trying to block. But he knocked aside the second punch and tripped her.

Farrell caught her and lifted her back onto her feet as Lem yelled and charged in from the right just as a big bearded man bellowed, shoving past Rowena and slamming a haymaker at

Gar's jaw. Gar ducked; the haymaker caught Lem and sent him flying. Then Gar hooked a fist into the bearded man's belly. He doubled over, and Gar straightened him with an uppercut.

He saw Farrell swinging from the side and shot to his feet, blocking the punch, but Zeke darted in past Farrell, head down, butting Gar in the belly.

Gar fell backward, and boots swung at his head. He caught the first and turned, pulling it with him. The bandit woman yelped and stumbled over him, tripping and falling straight into the kicking boots of her fellows. They shouted in surprise and pulled their feet back as Gar pushed himself up.

A huge weight struck his shoulders and slammed him back to the ground. Boots swung at his head, and Gar decided it was time for telekinesis. He caught the boots with his mind and swung them high. Their startled owners brayed as they fell, but other boots were slamming into his legs, and whoever it was on his back sat up long enough to hammer a punch at the back of his head.

The world blurred, and Gar hung onto consciousness grimly, thinking of that same hammer shooting up from beneath the ape on his back. He heard a startled contralto cry and the weight lessened. He shoved himself up, jolting his rider off, and scrambled to his feet in a small clearing among the circle of boots—the outlaws had given the rider room. Now they pressed in, roaring and eager.

But only eight of them could get close enough to swing at him. They moved in, shoulder to shoulder, forming a circle, so no matter how many were waiting their turn, he only had to worry about the front rank.

Having started using telekinesis, Gar saw no reason to stop. He swung and kicked, grabbed shirts and turned, hurling their owners into their mates, then spun back to block the next punch. More than a few made it through his guard; pain burned in his side and back and flank, but he stayed on his feet and kept chopping, though his arms grew heavy as lead and weary,

weary. They would wear him down, he realized with a sinking heart, then bucked his spirits up; they would know they'd been in a fight!

Finally a voice soared high over the tumult: "H-O-O-O-L-D!"

The clansfolk slowed, then stilled, glaring at Gar with fists raised, but waiting. Gar stopped, too, fists high, chest heaving like a race horse's at the end of a run.

The outlaws parted and Rowena strode through. "All right, you can keep your pack." She turned to her people. "He fought well and he fought clean, and what good will it do us to kick him to bits?"

" 'Specially since he might kick one or two of *us* into the long sleep first," the bearded man grunted.

"Could be, Clem, and I'd hate to lose you," Rowena returned.

Somebody chuckled in the crowd.

Rowena turned and clapped Gar on the arm. "Good enough, stranger. You're one of us, if you want to be—and if not, we'll trade for your goods, if you like anything we've got."

Gar felt the change in the emotions of the people around him, saw grins breaking out through puffy lips, and lowered his fists, though he still remained wary. "You folks keep the furs that you skin off your game, don't you?"

"That we do, and a'many of them are pretty to behold," Rowena confirmed, "though I don't know if it's worth putting off a new coat for a year, just to have something to trade for your pins and pretties."

Gar shrugged. "You'll have to look for yourselves." He caught up his pack and sat on his heels, unbuckling the flap and letting it fall. Necklaces of synthetic gems gleamed in the sunlight, packets of needles and pins winked, and a breeze wafted the scent of his spice packets to the outlaws. Some exclaimed with delight, others groaned with longing, and Gar felt so sorry for the poor folk who lived so hard an existence that such simple luxuries as these could brighten their lives so much, that he felt a strong impulse to give them away. Only an impulse, and he choked it quickly; without trade goods, he'd have no excuse to wander from clan to clan with impunity. Instead he said, "Let's take them over by your cottages and you can show me what you have to trade."

The outlaws agreed with shouts of approval and turned away to their cottages.

Rowena stayed by Gar, grinning. "Seems they've taken a liking to you, stranger."

"Gar," he said. "Gar Pike."

Rowena frowned. "Never heard of any Pike clan."

"We're from far away," Gar said, "very far."

"And so are your goods, belike. Well, they'd better be worth what my people bring you in trade—not gems that turn to slime in the rain, or needles that break on the first stitch."

"Oh, my goods will last," Gar assured her, "a very long time." After all, he had some notion of how well Herkimer's synthesizing machines had made them.

A voice from the roadside trees called, "Stop right there, stranger!"

Alea stopped, turning toward the sound. "I'm a peddler. Anything to trade?"

"A peddler?" The voice couldn't hide its eagerness. Brush rustled, and two clansfolk stepped onto the road from either side, their rifles lowering. The woman said, "Not too safe traveling alone, you know."

Alea shrugged. "Sometimes it's not too safe traveling in company, either." At the woman's frown, she explained, "It depends on your companion."

"I reckon that makes sense," the woman said. "Why, you don't even carry a rifle!"

Alea shrugged. "What good would it do me? As you say, people don't travel alone. What good is one rifle against two—or five or six?"

"Better than none," the man said, frowning.

"Worse than none," Alea countered. "If people see you're unarmed, they know you mean no harm."

The man and woman exchanged a glance. "She's got a point," the man allowed.

"She has," the woman said, and turned back to Alea. "I'm Hazel Gregor."

"Alea Larsdatter." Alea proffered a hand.

Hazel took it. "We have furs and pretty pebbles to trade, and if you don't want any of those, at least we can give you dinner and a bed for the night. Come on along to the Big House, now, and let's see what you've got to trade with."

"Thank you." Alea relaxed a little and followed her back to their homestead, leaving the man on guard.

More sentries stepped out, alert and with rifles at the ready, as Alea and Hazel came up the track toward the house. When they saw Hazel, though, they waved and faded back into the shrubbery.

"Are they always on guard?" Alea asked.

"No, we take turns," Hazel said. "We change the guard every four hours."

"All your lives?"

"Of course," Hazel said, surprised. "We wouldn't want the Mahons to catch us napping."

Alea thought of spending her life that way and hid a shudder.

The Big House shouldered up above the trees, and Alea wondered why they called it "big." It couldn't have been more than fifty feet long, with two stories and an attic. Then they came past the trees and Alea saw the dozen single-story dwellings clustered around it in a circle, and understood. None could have been wider than twenty feet.

"The married folk live in the small houses?"

Hazel nodded. "Grandma and Grandpa live in the Big House with the bachelor folk and widowed ones. Keeps everybody more in line, and the old folks don't get lonely."

Alea wondered how impatient the young folk became, wondered also if any married simply to gain homes of their own.

They came into the grassy circle between the houses to find two cows grazing amid sheep and goats. Boys and girls of ten and twelve stood watch over them, looking bored, with the help of a few dogs. Older men and women were doing chores—planing boards, polishing rifles, churning butter, casting bullets, and so on. They looked up with interest at the stranger. Then they saw the pack on her back, dropped their tools, and hurried forward.

They converged on the double door of the big house. "She a peddler?" asked a sixtyish man.

"That I am," Alea replied. "What have you to trade?"

"Some carvings," the old man said.

A woman near him said, "Carvings indeed! They're the sweetest statues you'll ever see. Me, I've some pretty pebbles I've been saving for a necklace. You go on in, missy, and I'll run and find them."

"I'll be eager to see them," Alea said politely, then went through the door.

They came into the keeping room—a central chamber about thirty feet long and twenty wide, furnished with plain wooden chairs and tables, lovingly finished with a glow that betokened many hours of rubbing with oil and wax. They had an economy of design, sweeping planes and flowing curves that took Alea's breath away. A few chairs were cushioned, and the armchair by the fire was padded and upholstered, for in it sat an old man with white beard and hair, wrinkled face, and keen bright eyes that inspected Alea thoroughly at a glance and delivered a verdict on her suitability to be in Grandpa's house. Apparently the verdict was positive, because the old man said, "Welcome, stranger."

Hazel led Alea over to him. "Grandpa, this is Alea. She's a peddler."

"And a brave one, if she takes to the roads by herself with no rifle," Grandpa said.

Hazel turned to Alea. "This is Grandpa Esau Gregor."

"Welcome in my home," the old man said. "What kind of pretties have you brought us, child?"

"Oh, ribbons and pins and needles," Alea said. "Some nutmeg, too, and cinnamon and pepper. Then there's jewelry from some clans I've traded with, and pretty pots and cups."

"Don't know as how another clan can do any better than my own children," Grandpa opined, "but it's nice to have a reminder that there are other folks out there besides the Mahons." He grimaced at the name. "Let's see your stock."

Alea gladly shrugged out of her pack and lowered it to the hearth as the clansfolk gathered around. She was just opening the buckles when she heard the groan.

The outlaws crowded close to admire and touch. One young man hung back, though. He was tall and lean, looking to be made of whipcord—whipcord and straw, for his hair was so pale as to be nearly white. But his jacket was made of leather, fringed and decorated with colored quills, and he held a half-fletched arrow in one hand and a small knife in the other, as though he had come running in the middle of a task.

"Take a look!" Gar called to him. "Do I have anything you'd want to trade for?"

"Yeah, Kerlew," one of the women said, her tone mocking, "you'd best sniff the spices, since all you're fit for is cooking."

Kerlew flushed.

"Be fair, Elise," Rowena said, but she smiled. "He's a dab hand with a needle, too, and the peddler's got plenty of those."

Gar frowned. "Who elected him chief cook and bottlewasher?"

"Why, what else can he do?" Elise jibed. "He's a coward!"

"Too scared even to go hunting for anything bigger 'n a squirrel," another outlaw agreed, "though he doesn't mind skinning the beasts and tanning their hides, so we know it's not being squeamish about death."

Kerlew reddened more. "There's a deal of difference between *killing* a deer and taking its coat, Enoch!"

"Oh, sure," Enoch said. "Not much danger of being gored by an antler, when you're skinning one that's already dead."

"He knows how to hide good, though, don't he?" another man jibed.

"And how to duck," Elise agreed.

"How well does he fight if you're attacked?" Gar asked quietly.

An uncomfortable silence settled over the clearing. Then Rowena said, "The clans haven't come against us yet, peddler, but that's what got you cast out in the first place, isn't it, Kerlew? Refusing to go out to fight the Gainty clan."

"I fought well enough when they ambushed us!" Kerlew retorted.

"Oh, aye, when it was kill or be killed," Enoch sneered. "Sure, you fought like a cornered rat."

"So," Gar said, still quietly, "you have no problem with defending yourself and your clan—only with visiting death and misery on your neighbors."

"So I said," Kerlew said hotly, "and for that they cast me out! Why would I turn against people now that I'm outcast?"

"Why, for a living, boy," Lem said impatiently.

"I can find enough nuts and berries for that," Kerlew retorted, "aye, and kill to eat, if I have to."

"You just don't like the feel of it when they die, do you?" Gar asked.

Kerlew reddened again. "There's enough dying already. Why add to it?"

Gar wondered if the boy was a latent telepath.

"Not much point in keeping one like that around, is there?" Rowena asked Gar. "But we won't cast him out. Outlawing once is bad enough, but outlawing from outlaws?"

"Any who need shelter with us should have it," Elise agreed.

"That's very charitable of you," Gar said slowly.

Kerlew turned crimson and started a retort.

"But he will fight if the clans come against you," Gar said, "you've heard him say so—and if they do, you'll need every rifle you can muster."

The outlaws fell silent, staring at him in surprise, and Rowena turned thoughtful.

"There's this, too," Gar said. "You never know which 'weakling' will turn out to have the Second Sight—or even a gift for magic, if it comes to that."

Kerlew stared at him, amazed, and some of the outlaws muttered to one another, caught between superstition and mockery.

Rowena demanded, "You really think there's magic?"

Gar remembered meeting the fairies. "Doesn't everybody?"

"Never seen any, myself," Farrell scoffed, but his look was uncertain.

"Well, if it's real, show us some," Lem said to Kerlew. "Go on, boy—tell us what's happening at, say, the Gregors' homestead."

The outlaws recovered from their superstitious awe with laughs and jeers. "Yeah, you tell us, Kerlew boy!"

"Aye! If you've got magic, tell us what's happening there!"

"Or make a squirrel fall out of that tree smack dab into the cooking pot!"

"Hey, I can do that." Farrell lifted his rifle and sighted at the tree limb, then lowered it, shaking his head. "Don't need no magic. No, I like him telling us what's happening at the Gregors' house."

The clansfolk cast a few surreptitious glances at Farrell, and Gar realized the man was himself a Gregor and eager for news of home, though he would never admit it.

"Yeah, see twenty miles for us, Kerlew!" a young woman jibed. "What're they doing at the Gregor house?"

"And none of this saying they're sitting down to dinner, mind you—anyone could guess that, at sunset!"

Kerlew grew redder and redder at the mockery and finally burst out, "All right, blast you! Just shut up and let me look!" He closed his eyes and sat, rigid as a pole, hands clasping his knees.

The catcalls cut off as though a valve had closed and the outlaws stared at him, taken aback. Then superstitious dread began to show in a face here and there.

Gar braced himself, readying a vision to implant in the boy's mind. He knew he'd been riding a bluff and would have to make good on it.

Alea looked up at the groan, eyes wide. "Who's in pain?"

"Oh, that's Linda," one of the men said, his face resigned. "The baby's fine, but we might lose her."

"Lose her?" Alea leaped up. "Why? What happened?"

"She lost a lot of blood," Hazel said, frowning. "We managed to stop it, but likely too late." She shook her head sadly. "She's wasting away, but what can anyone do?"

"Help her body to make more blood, that's what!" Alea turned toward the groan and started walking. "Take me to her!"

The crowd parted in surprise but didn't look hopeful. Hazel hurried after her. "She's in her room, that third door, but you can't make blood, Alea."

"No, but her body can."

Hazel skipped ahead and opened the door, holding up a hand to caution Alea. She poked her head in, then back out and beckoned. With soft steps, they went into the room.

There was a fire on the hearth, but the woman who lay in the bed shivered nonetheless. Alea was shocked at the paleness of her face. A young man sat beside her, holding her hand; he looked up as Alea came in and she was shocked again by the suffering written there. His eyes were hollow and darkened, his skin pale and waxy. He looked as though he hadn't slept in days, and he probably hadn't. She could imagine him dozing off in the night and waking at Linda's slightest groan.

Alea touched the hand he was holding; Linda's skin felt like ice. She felt for the pulse and could barely find it.

Before Gar could implant a vision, Kerlew spoke, voice sounding as though it drifted wind-borne from a thousand miles away.

"There's a woman there, a stranger, and she's sitting in a bedroom holding a younger woman's hand. Poor soul, she's pale as milk, and there's a young fellow sitting by with his head in his hands."

The outlaws stared.

Kerlew's eyes flew open in alarm. "Did I say that?"

"You did," Gar said before anyone else could speak. He turned to Farrell. "Who would the young woman be?"

Farrell had to lick his lips before he could answer. "Might be Linda Balfour. She was betrothed to Martin before I . . . left, and we was supposed to meet his bodyguards halfway to take her on home. That was when we saw the Mahon boys swimming, and I spoke against an ambush 'cause it weren't what we'd been sent to do." He shook his head angrily, as though to banish the memory. "If they married, she'd likely have been heavy with child last spring, and light by now."

The outlaws stared at Kerlew with awe and dread.

The lad trembled. "I never! Never done that before, never seen!" He rounded on Farrell. "And wouldn'ta done it now, if it hadn't been for your yammering!"

"Oh, yes you have," said another, "for there's more 'n once you've wakened all the bachelor's house with your shouting to warn folks of ambush."

"Those was dreams!"

"Second-sight dreams," a third young man said, eyeing Kerlew with respect but no friendliness.

"Yes," Gar said, "it seems that I spoke more truly than I knew, though perhaps you saw clearly now because the young woman's heart was calling out for any who could help her." But Gar knew it wasn't the sick woman who had been broadcasting anxiety—it was Alea, for she was the young woman sitting by the bedside.

"What color hair did the young man have?" Farrell asked.

"What? . . . Why, yellow." Kerlew jammed his jaw shut, looking alarmed at his own words.

"Martin's hair is yellow," Farrell said heavily.

Rowena nodded. "Most folks have red or brown."

"But—but I ain't no seer!" Kerlew protested. "I ain't no Druid!"

"Perhaps not, but you seem to have the talent for it." Gar turned to Rowena. "I'd treat him well, if I were you. If he practices, he might be able to learn how to eavesdrop on all the clans about here, and be able to tell you if anyone starts agitating to band together and move against you."

"Either that, or send him to the Druids," Lem said.

"No-o-o-o!" Kerlew clutched his scalp. "No, I don't want it! Get it out of my head!"

"There's few who do want it," Gar said gently, "for it's as much a torment as a blessing—but it can help your friends greatly."

Kerlew stilled, then bowed his head, though he kept his fingers in his hair. "I wouldn't use it to harm any travelers—nor any clan!"

"So long as you use it to help us." Rowena laid a hand on his knee. "You've always said you weren't a coward, Kerlew, just sick of killing. Well, now's your chance to prove it."

The lad raised his head from his hands, frowning. "Prove it how?"

"By learning to control this gift, and use it for the good of the band," Gar told him.

"He just can't stand the sight of blood," someone said.

Kerlew turned toward the voice, face hardening. "It ain't the blood, Jeeter, and it ain't the pain and the writhing, and the wounded screaming for someone to take pity on them and kill them. No, it's the wife left to grieve and live on the clan's charity the rest of her days, and the children crying for their daddy and never understanding why he'll never come home again." His eyes began to burn. "It's the girls in pigtails who can't understand why their daddy would go to the Afterworld instead of coming home to them, and the barefoot boys who can't understand how the gods can be good if they let their mommies die." His eyes blazed, his voice deepened and boomed as he said, "It ain't the killing and the dying that anger me so much as the birthing and the living that has to go on in the shadow it casts over them all!"

The outlaws were silent a minute, staring at Kerlew as though they'd never seen him before. Then Rowena cleared her throat and said, "Yes. I'll allow as how the boy has some magic."

And Kerlew stood stunned, unable to believe that voice and those words had come out of his own mouth.

The sick woman opened her eyes, uncomprehending.

"Who are you?" the young man croaked.

"A stranger," Alea said, "and a friend." She turned to Hazel. "You're right—it's blood loss. I think she's picked up a fever, too."

"Childbed fever," Hazel sighed. "Happens too often, I fear."

"Too often indeed, but you have fruit juice, don't you? And liver."

"Well, we've apples," Hazel said in surprise, "and cider, of course. We can get liver soon enough, if you think she needs it."

"Cow's liver is best, though that of pigs or chickens will do," Alea told her. "Tell someone to start boiling it for broth, and we'll spoon it into her. In the meantime, let's try that cider."

"Hard or soft?"

"Soft, definitely soft! Hurry, Hazel—we may not have much time." She turned to the young man. "Get you to bed. You can't do anything for her, and we'll waken you if she gets worse."

"I won't leave her," the young man said stubbornly. "She could pass any minute."

"Not yet," Alea said, "not if she can still groan." Then she relented and said, "You can make up your pallet right here, so you can be beside her if she needs you, but you're no help to her exhausted."

The young man tried to hold her gaze, but his own strayed back to Linda. "You talk sense, I guess. Well, I'll go get blankets." He rose stiffly, then held out a hand. "Thank you. I'm Martin."

"And I'm Alea." She took his hand. "Go get your blankets."

• • •

By dinnertime, Linda had absorbed half a gallon of cider and been able to sip two bowlfuls of salted broth, and Martin was so soundly asleep he didn't waken at the sound of feet moving to and from the bed. Alea sat by Linda in his place, mind reaching into the young mother's body, to stimulate blood production, but feeling very helpless nonetheless.

Hazel came in. "Time to come to dinner, Alea."

"I'll wait."

"No, you'll go now," Hazel insisted. "*I'll* wait. Tell me what signs to watch for."

Alea shrugged. "There isn't much—only if she begins to get some color back, and we probably won't see that until tomorrow. Keep a cold cloth on her forehead, though. If her breath gets much more shallow or her pulse fades, call me right away."

"I will," Hazel promised. "Get you to supper, now, and then sleep, for I imagine you'll be up with her the whole night if we let you."

"I'll want to take the midnight watch, at least." Alea rose unwillingly.

"We'll see to it she's tended, and call you if there's any change for the worse." Hazel shooed her toward the door. "It's good of you to care so for someone who isn't one of your own."

Alea stopped and turned back, looking her in the eye. "We're all each other's own, Hazel—every woman in the world."

Hazel gave her a long silent look, then nodded. "We'll see what you have to say about the men if she gets better. Eat now, for you'll need your nourishment as much as she does."

Alea woke on her pallet by the hearth and saw a girl of about twelve kneeling nearby, feeding small sticks to a shrunken fire. She glanced at Alea, saw her open eyes, and smiled shyly. "Morning, Miss Alea."

"Good morning," Alea said, and was about to ask the girl's name when a knock sounded at the door. They both turned to stare at it. The girl said, "Only strangers knock."

Three clansfolk hurried to the door with rifles ready but not leveled. An older man pulled it open, stared in surprise. "Versey!" He turned to call to the people inside, "It's Versey the Druid!" Then he turned back, pushing the door wide and bowing the visitor into the house. "Be welcome, Reverend!"

Alea stared and held her breath, waiting for a tall, white-haired man with a long beard and a snowy robe, with a golden sickle at his belt and mistletoe in his hair.

8

"May Lugh's light shine on all in this house," Versey said, stepping in, and Alea was very much disappointed. Here was no august holy presence, but an ordinary middle-aged man in woolen jacket and baggy trousers, pulling a wide-brimmed hat from his head. He had a beard, but it was trimmed short and grizzled, as was his close-cropped hair. He looked like any of the clansmen, except that his jacket was dove gray instead of plaid.

Hazel came hurrying out of the sickroom, waving another woman in. She bustled up to Versey, wiping her hands on her apron. "Be welcome, Druid! What news?"

"Why, only that Linda's at death's door," Versey said. "The whole valley knows it."

Hazel's face hardened. "Yes, I suppose a Mahon sentry might have eavesdropped on someone from the house talking about it—and if one Mahon heard, they'd all know in an hour, and the whole valley by the end of the day."

"As they should," the Druid said firmly. "The danger of one is the danger of all."

"Well, I'll agree with that," one of the men said, "but not the way you mean."

"I'll settle for any agreement at all," Versey sighed. "I'll pay my respects to your grandfather, if I may."

"Surely, Reverend!" Hazel turned to discover most of the clan surrounding her. They opened an avenue to the hearth and the old man's great chair beside it.

Versey strode down that alley and gave Grandpa a small bow. "The gods keep your house safe, Esau!"

"And may they keep the wind at your back, Versey," Grandpa said. "Come to join us for the deathwatch, have you?"

Alea couldn't help herself. "She's not going to die."

They both turned to stare at her. Then storm clouds gathered in Grandpa's face, anger warring with ingrained courtesy toward a guest, but Versey said, "I've not seen you before. Who be you, lady?"

Hazel stepped forward. "This is Alea, a peddler—only she seems to know something of healing, too, and has been doing what she can for our Linda."

Alea shrank inside. One way not to get along with the local priest and healer was to set up in competition with him.

But Versey seemed interested, not antagonized. "For loss of blood? What have you been doing, then?"

"Feeding her soft cider," Alea said, "for it's sweet, and the blood carries sweetening to the rest of the body."

"And it's wet, like blood, so it might help fill up the veins." Versey nodded. "What else?"

"Broth," Alea said, "of liver, to strengthen the blood."

"And water, again to fill the veins." Versey nodded. "It may work, if we can keep her alive long enough for the heart to fill her veins again." He turned back to Grandpa. "It may be that I haven't come for a wake, after all. May I pay Linda a visit?"

"If you think it will do any good, Versey, of course," Grandpa said, somewhat unwillingly.

"Thank you, Esau." Versey gave the old man a bit of a bow, then turned back to Alea. "Show me, young woman."

Alea led him to Linda's room, reflecting that the Druids had come down in the world very badly. Instead of the household bowing to him, showing him deference, and clinging to his slightest pronouncements, they treated him with courtesy only, and seemed to be happy to see him because he was a visitor, not because he was a holy man.

Versey sat down by the bed and took Linda's hand. He inspected it closely. "The nails look well enough, though pale. The skin is dry and flaking, but that's what you'd expect with so much blood loss." He touched her wrist and gazed off into space for a few minutes, and Alea realized he was taking Linda's pulse. He nodded. "Slow but strong." He looked down at the sleeping face. "She breathes lightly but easily. So pale, though! Is her color any better than it was yesterday?"

Alea studied her patient closely. "Not really, but I keep hoping."

Versey nodded. "She may yet live."

"What else can we do?" Alea burst out.

Versey shrugged. "The ancients used to pour blood from one person into another, but even if we could work out the manner of it, the blood might be wrong. There are different kinds of blood, you see, and we've lost the knack of telling the one from the other."

Alea flirted with the idea of calling Herkimer for directions on blood typing, but decided against it; she might be handing Linda from a natural death to burning for witchcraft. Herself, too, of course. "There must be something!"

"There are some herbs that night help, in that broth of yours." Versey rose. "I'll see what these Gregors have by way of a garden." Briefly, he rested a hand on her shoulder. "Don't worry, daughter. She'll live, or I mistake the signs. You've done well, very well indeed."

Then he left, and Alea stared after him, wondering why he had called her "daughter" when he hadn't said that to any of the others.

• • •

After dinner, while others watched Linda, Versey and Alea talked shop. He told her which herbs were good for what ills, and little verses to help her remember. She, in turn, told him about the minor operations she had studied, and the importance of cleanliness for surgery. That led to germ theory, and she was surprised and delighted that Versey already knew of it, though he spoke of germs as creatures carried by the blood, so small that no one could see them and that could live on doorknobs or dishes or any surface. He sighed as he told Alea of his trials in trying to persuade the clans to be clean. He had even told them of brownies and fairies, and how they hated dirt and laziness. Questioning, she discovered that he truly believed in the spirits and remembering the fairies she and Gar had met, she could see why.

"You've heard that some of those tiny creatures you call 'germs' grow in our stomachs and help us digest our food, of course," he said.

Alea was amazed how much knowledge had survived the collapse of the colony's technological civilization. "Yes." She smiled. "They live on a little of our food, and help our bodies to use it."

Versey smiled, too. "That seems fair." He turned to look at Linda's door, worry creasing his forehead. "She could use some more of them now, I don't doubt. The heat of the fever has probably killed a good many of them."

"Of course!" Alea said with chagrin. "Yogurt! Why didn't I think of that?"

Versey turned back to her in surprise. "Yogurt?"

"Sour milk left on the stove overnight," Alea explained, "with the fire banked inside. It will pick up spores from the air and clabber. When it becomes—well, almost like butter—it's sour but good to eat, and has bac . . . the same kind of tiny creatures as those in our stomachs."

"A good thought." Versey rose. "I'll ask Hazel to set a bowl of milk on the stove."

"And tomatoes!" Alea reached up to catch his sleeve. "I

should have thought of that. We must give her tomato juice to drink!"

"Red as blood, and the same consistency." Versey nodded. "Like calls to like, and it will bring blood into being. Very good, Alea. I should have thought of that, too."

He went off to the kitchen, and Alea scolded herself for forgetting. The fever and the blood loss had both doubtless depleted Linda of electrolytes. She'd thought that at first and been angry because there were no oranges or lemons here, but they had served tomatoes at dinner, and she'd forgotten that tomatoes had citric acid! Not the best electrolyte, to be sure, but enough.

"They'll see to it." Versey smiled as he came back to her. "How did you learn of healing, Alea? I've never before met a peddler who knew anything of it. Did you learn it as a child?"

Time to be vague but truthful. "No, I learned it from a traveling companion. He'd been a soldier, so I suppose he learned it from a battlefield healer."

"A healer on the battlefield!" Versey sighed. "Wouldn't it be good if the clans had something of the sort!"

"Well, they do seem to know a little," Alea said cautiously. "Are you the only healer in this region?"

"In the county, at least," Versey said, shaking his head. "It would be good if there were more Druids, and if all of us learned healing, but it's a hard life, enduring the hidden contempt of those you try to save."

"Save?" Alea asked in surprise.

Versey gave her a sad smile. "The healer in me tries to save their bodies from death, Alea, and the priest in me tries to save their souls from dedication to killing and cruelty. But no one believes in the gods, not really, so they don't respect the few of us who do."

"Then why do you?" Alea asked, wondering.

"Well, I was raised knowing the old tales," Versey said. "Parents tell them to their children at bedtime, and around the fire on long winter nights. But as you grow up, you learn that everyone really thinks they're just that, stories—stories that teach you right from wrong and how to steer clear of the worst mistakes you can make—but only stories for all that."

"Then what made you believe them?"

"Despair." Versey looked straight into her eyes.

Alea stared.

"I despaired of the killing ever coming to an end," Versey explained. "I despaired of clans ever learning to forgive one another for their ancestors' crimes and for the murdering that's gone on ever since. I cast about for some way to end it, someone who could tell them 'Stop!' and make it happen and finally realized that only the gods could do that. If they would. That's when I began to believe in them."

"But if they can, why don't they?" Alea asked.

"I understood that, too," Versey said. "It all came to me in an instant that made me feel as though something, someone, was pulling me up by the hair. I realized that the gods must be real, but that they won't make the clans stop, only tell them how."

"The clans won't listen, though," Alea protested.

"No, they won't." Versey heaved a gusty sigh. "They won't, though I've spent my life trying to tell them. 'The gods are real,' that's my message—the gods are real, and they're talking to you all the time, if you'll only stop and listen."

"I've listened," Alea said. "I haven't heard."

"Haven't you?" Versey's eyes lit with zeal. "These are the gods of the forest, remember, the gods of field and brook, of thunder and rain, of rock and earth and all that grows from it. Haven't you ever gone out to the fields and simply sat and listened?"

"Of course I have," Alea said, "when people become too much for me."

"Then you've heard the wind as it blows through the corn," Versey said, "and the water as it runs in the brook. You've heard birdsong and thunder and the fallen leaves rustling as you walk through the forest in autumn."

"Yes, of course." Alea blinked. "Who hasn't?"

"You've heard all that, and you say you've never heard the gods talking?" Versey leaned toward her with a smile of pity. "Listen again, lass, listen with your heart as well as your ears, and you'll know suddenly what the gods want of you. You won't hear it in words, just with a sudden certainty, here . . ."—he touched his temple—". . . and here . . ."—he touched his heart—". . . a certainty, and all at once you'll be sure what's right and wrong." He leaned back, hands on his knees, beaming. "*Then* it's time for words—to tell it to other folk."

"But they'll say I'm crazed, that my mind is shattered!"

"Not if they listen, too," Versey said, his smile telling her that they now shared a great treasure. "Not if you can talk them into listening, too."

Gar's pack bulged by the time he was done trading; pelts and furs take up a great deal more room than needles and spices. Well, Herkimer could always use more furs to fashion clothing for the next cold-weather planet they might visit. Gar would simply have to arrange another drop and send the furs back up with the drone that brought him more trade goods. Certainly none of the clans would want more pelts; they all trapped enough on their own. At least the outlaws had found some gold nuggets to trade—not that they would bring much from the next clan down the road. They might do for fashioning buttons, or even jewelry, but the clansfolk didn't really seem to have any concept of money.

Trading done, they all sat around a fire in the center of the circle of cottages, watching the spit turn the carcass of the day's game—a wild boar. Gar looked from Rowena on his right to Lem on his left and wondered why they bothered waylaying travelers if they had no use for money. Needles and pins, perhaps?

"Penny for your thoughts, peddler," Rowena said.

"A penny?" Gar looked up, startled. "You have pennies?"

Rowena turned wary. "Of course, but don't think you can

talk us into trading them away. Everyone knows you need pennies to lay on the eyes of the dead."

"Oh." Gar pursed his lips in thought. "So that's what they're for?"

"Of course!" Rowena stared. "What would *you* use them for?"

"Trading," Gar said quickly.

Rowena gave a laugh that was more like a grunt. "Fools they'd be who traded them away. How would they bury their dead, then? That must be why the ancients made so many pennies—because they knew everyone must die some day."

"Is that why you waylay travelers, then?" Gar asked. "In hopes they'll have pennies?"

"Who'd be so foolish as to bring their dead-coins with them on a journey?" Rowena countered.

"Peddlers," Gar said, "like me. You must have a lot of us come through your woods, if you find us worth ambushing."

Rowena looked at him strangely. "Peddlers are even more rare than pennies, stranger, and don't try to tell me you don't know it! No, most of the traffic is the escort parties a clan sends to take a Druid or bard from one clan to another, or their young folk on wander-year, and you may be sure we give each one a wide berth."

"Then who do you rob?"

Rowena shrugged. "There's the occasional Druid or bard who's as cocky as you, thinking he or she can fight off a whole outlaw band—though they mostly have less reason." She gave him a sardonic smile. "You didn't fare so badly. If all travelers fought like you, we'd have to send every outlaw against them, every time."

"Thanks for the compliment," Gar said. "Peddlers don't rate armed escorts, though?"

"More than any Druid or healer!" Rowena said. "Fact is, they're so prized that no clan will risk hurting them." The sardonic smile was still there. "That'd be cause enough to start a new feud."

"So a peddler alone is a real find," Lem put in.

"Yes, I can see I must have been," Gar said slowly. "Too tempting to resist." He looked around him at gaunt faces with the sores of scurvy and other vitamin deficiencies. They watched the roasting boar with gleaming, hungry eyes. "You can't farm among these trees, can you?"

"No, and if we cleared land for a field, it would tell the clansfolk where to look," Lem confirmed. " 'See here! Outlaws near! Come and get 'em!' "

Rowena nodded. "They won't miss a few sheep, or the odd cow now and then—but a dozen sheep at a time, or a cow a week? That would bring the whole clan marching against us."

"I wouldn't think any clan would risk a pitched battle against so strong a band. Why, there must be sixty of you! And in your own forest?"

"Oh we might win—once," Rowena said. "Trouble is, they wouldn't stay gone. They'd come back—and back, and back, and back. We'd start another feud, and that's what we've fled."

Gar looked again at the people around him and felt renewed determination to find a way to end the fighting.

Gar declined several offers of hospitality, saying that he felt hemmed in by houses, and rolled out his blanket by the communal fire. He wasn't fooling anyone—the outlaws all knew he had reason not to trust them.

Of course, by the same token, he didn't dare sleep, so he sat cross-legged on the blanket, recited a koan, and let himself fall into a trance that would give his body some rest but also leave him aware of his surroundings. He knew he would have to find a shelter for a nap the next day, but he wasn't about to leave himself vulnerable just then.

When the waking sleep had taken hold, and the outlaws' village seemed remote, as though he saw it through a pane of thickened glass, Gar let his awareness expand to embrace the myriad of thoughts and emotions from the animals of the forest—hunger and greed, fear and the excitement of the chase, lust and frustration—then farther and farther, eavesdropping for a few seconds on the dreams of each of the homesteads around the forest. There, finally, he found the waking mind he sought.

How was your day, Alea?

Gar! Thank heavens! she thought back, then poured out the tale of the Gregor clan and Linda's near-death—not in words, but in a rush of emotions and images that lasted only seconds.

Then you saved another life? Well done!

How could I do less? Alea thought, abashed.

No, that's not your way. His thoughts warmed in a way that made her both yearn and shrink. Gar must have sensed it, for he overlaid the heat with a layer of seeming coolness. *Because of that, you seem to have won the approval of the family Druid.*

Approval, and a great deal of knowledge. Alea sent another tumble of images and concepts that summarized all Versey had told her about his life, and his place in a society built on feuding. Finally she asked, *What of you? Where are you? Not alone in the forest, I hope!*

In the forest, but not alone. Now it was Gar's turn for the cascade of emotions, images, and ideas that had made up his day.

When he was done, Alea asked, *So the clans assign escort parties to peddlers? Wouldn't it have been handy to know that!*

It would, Gar answered, *but if I had, I wouldn't have come to know as much about the outlaws as I do.*

Yes. Fancy being outlawed for pleading the cause of peace!

Would-be peacemakers have been declared criminals before this. Gar's thought carried a tone of resignation. *I've even heard of them being jailed during wartime.*

How ironic! The killers are honored and the peace-lovers are despised! What of the thieves and murderers and adulterers?

If they murder someone within their own clan, they're outlawed, Gar returned. *As to the others, as long as their crimes are directed against the enemy clan, they're applauded.*

So the feuds turn everything upside down, Alea mused. *What if there were no war? Would it be turned right-side up?*

Let us cause an outbreak of peace and find out, Gar suggested.

There was a little more, an exchange of personal reactions to the day, but Alea's thoughts grew more and more bleary with sleepiness, and Gar told her good night. The conversation over, he sat and listened to the silence for a while.

Suddenly, a current seemed to pass from the crown of his head down his skin to his toes, and a distant voice seemed to call, *Magnus! Where do you wander? Speak, my brother!*

Gar answered with a silent surge of joy. *Gregory! How fare you?*

Instantly, he sensed the turbulence, the yearning, the fear, the abject conviction of worthlessness when Gregory looked at the glowing face of the beautiful woman who lay sleeping before him.

You are in love! Gar had to suppress the feeling that he had never thought it could happen to his bookish little brother. Then his own thoughts darkened. *Wait! I know that face!*

We sit in judgment over her, Gregory mourned. *You must join us in rendering that verdict, Magnus.*

Gar listened, spellbound, as the story flooded him, heart and mind. He responded with panic, quickly allayed into wariness, and finally into wholehearted approval and good wishes—but also cautions.

Then his mother, his sister, and his middle brother each added their good wishes, modulated onto Gregory's. At last his little brother said good-bye and the contact was broken.

Little! Little no longer! In love, his humanity restored, and likely to propose. Gar sat galvanized with apprehension, then remembered his mother's sage counsel and let it ebb . . .

And felt far more alone than he had in two years.

In the morning, Linda actually woke up and smiled. She was still too weak to hold her new baby, but her eyes spoke volumes as she gazed at the little bundle in Hazel's arms. Alea watched and marveled that a woman could go through so much pain, bring herself to death's door, knock, and manage to run away—and still think it all worthwhile!

"She has a reason for living now," Versey explained to her

after breakfast, as they sat outside on the bench beside the door.

"But she's so young!" Alea protested. "Surely she had reason enough already, especially with her husband! Or aren't they in love?"

"You saw them look at one another this morning, and how he caressed her hand," Versey answered. "Yes, that's reason to live—for the moment. It doesn't give you any stake in the future, though."

His words echoed inside Alea, in a hollow she tried to ignore. To hide it again, she asked, "What's your reason for living, then?"

"A wife and three children," Versey answered, "though I sometimes think she must have been crazed, to wed a man like me who must live on the leavings of others."

Alea stared. "But surely the people you tend provide for you!"

"Most of the time, they'd rather not even see me," Versey said with a sardonic smile. "If you don't believe in the gods, you'd rather not be reminded of them. Oh, each clan in the country will send me a pittance to make sure no other has a right to look down on them. We are the ones who keep the histories of our clans, after all, and remind them of their heritage."

"Surely they would listen carefully to you, then!"

"No one really pays much attention to the old ceremonies," Versey sighed. "The wandering bards, now, that's another matter. They're truly honored, since they bring news—and always compose a new ballad praising the valor of the clan who hosts them, every time they visit."

"Well, that's some respect for the old ways, at least," Alea said, "and the bards are trained much like Druids, aren't they?"

"Like it in that they learn all the old lore, and the craft of verse and lyric, aye. They know the stories of the gods, but not how to celebrate the rites."

"Well, I should think not! That's your province, and the clans have to come to you for that."

Versey shook his head. "The only time they send for me is when someone dies."

Shocked, Alea asked, "Not even when someone's ill?"

"You saw how it was with Linda." Versey nodded his head toward the doorway. "Two steps from her grave, she was, but did they call me? No. I heard the gossip and came for the death-watch."

"But . . . but . . . if they pay no heed to the ceremonies, why call you when someone dies?"

"That's the one rite they do want." Versey nodded sagely. "Believe in it or not, no one's about to take chances with the Afterlife. No, a Druid must come to the wake and say the prayers to speed the soul's journey to the Afterworld. And the folk must sing a coronach, a lament for the dead, if a bard's not at hand."

"What will happen if they don't?"

Versey shrugged. "Who knows? But I believe that without a Druid's testimony, the spirit of the dead would not be honored by his ancestors' ghosts. I believe it, and so do the clans—or if they don't, they're not about to take the risk. How much does it cost them, after all? A night and a day of mourning, and a smoked ham or bull's hide for the Druid. Why take the chance?"

"Why indeed?" Privately, Alea was shocked, though she tried not to show it. How could the Druid by so cynical and still fulfill his office?

Because his belief was stronger than his disillusionment, that was how—strong enough to allow him to cope with the facts, strong enough for him to live in reality.

"You'll be off peddling again, then?" Versey asked.

Alea nodded. "It's what I do."

"No it's not," Versey said.

Alea's heart skipped a beat. She stared at the Druid, wondering how he could have discovered that she was an off-planet agent.

But Versey wasn't looking back; he drained his mug and stood up. "You heal as well as trade, and it's as a healer you shall go when you leave this place. I'll speak to Esau and see you have a proper escort."

Alea nearly sagged with relief.

Versey was as good as his word. In spite of their cynicism, the clan still seemed to respect the Druid's words, for when Alea left the next morning, she left with gifts and lavish thanks—and a guard of a dozen clansfolk, to see her to the next homestead.

Gar strapped his pack shut and swung it up to his shoulders, then held out his hand to Rowena. "Thank you for your hospitality." He looked out at the assembled outlaws. "Thank you all."

They returned his thanks in chorus. Rowena smiled as she shook his hand. "Good luck on the road, peddler. We'd send an escort with you, but it would be more than likely to draw the anger of the next clan you met."

"Send me."

The crowd fell quiet, staring at the young man who stepped forward.

9

The outlaws all stared, astounded. Then Rowena found her voice. "Kerlew, are you sure?"

"Don't pretend you're sorry to see me go!" he said scornfully. "You've made it clear enough what you thought of me . . ." He looked around at the throng. "All of you."

"But we didn't know you were a seer," Rowena protested.

"Oh yes, that has made a difference!" Kerlew snapped. "Now instead of deriding me for cowardice, everyone shies away from me as though the Second Sight were catching! No, none of you will regret my going. That is . . ." he turned to Gar ". . . if you'll have me for a road companion."

"Gladly." Gar's thoughts hummed with plans for training the boy's psi talents. "I warn you, though, I'm not the most congenial company."

"Really! And I suppose you think I am?"

"No, I think I know you well enough for that." Gar grinned. "Fetch your pack, then, and let's be off."

Kerlew brought his backpack out from behind him. "It's here."

"Are you sure of this?" Rowena frowned. "We may give you

cold welcome here, Kerlew, but at least it's shelter."

"One companion will be enough." Kerlew gave her a harsh smile. "After all, is there any clan we could meet that will know me for what I am? No, I think I'll fare better as a trader."

"Then we'll send you with something to trade," Rowena said with sudden resolution, and turned to her band. "Everyone bring one thing, some small object that will do for a peddler! We can't let him go with empty hands!"

Fifteen minutes later, they strode into the forest. Kerlew carried a frame with two packs now, and the second held exquisite little carvings, polished semiprecious stones, and a few carefully wrapped porcelains.

"What songs do you know?" Gar asked.

"Songs?" Kerlew looked up in surprise. "Well, there's one about a hunter who's not very skilled."

"That will do," Gar said. "Let's have it."

Kerlew began to sing. After one verse, Gar recognized it and joined in on the chorus. Thus they strode off into the woodlands, roaring a song guaranteed to tell every outlaw and clan hunter for half a mile where they could find two wanderers.

Alea's escort were in a holiday mood, laughing and joking as they strolled down the dirt road. They kept a sharp eye for an ambush, but they weren't much worried; no clan would attack an escort party without asking their business. Seeing them prowl through the woods was one thing, but walking boldly down the road was entirely another; it generally meant that they were escorting someone, and anyone who would be escorted was sacrosanct. The Truce of Travel extended to return trips, too, so the Gregors weren't terribly concerned about mistakes.

But they weren't prepared for a single young woman, alone, who sat by the roadside on a boulder, watching and waiting.

She rose as the party neared. Something about her struck Alea—perhaps the sense of stillness about her, or the intentness with which her gaze fastened on the traveler-woman. Alea held up a hand. "Let's stop for a few minutes."

Agreeably, the party halted. Hazel raised a palm in greeting. "Good day to you, Moira."

"And to you, Hazel Gregor." But the young woman still stared at Alea.

Her gaze made Alea uncomfortable, but before she could say anything, Hazel asked in a half-joking manner, "Have you found these travelers whose coming you've been preaching about, the ones who will put an end to the feuding?"

"One of them," Moira said, staring directly into Alea's eyes. "One of them, yes."

Alarm thrilled through Alea, and before any of the Gregors could think about Moira's meaning, Alea said, "You've been foretelling the coming of peacemakers?"

"To all the clans," Moira said, "or as many as I can find. Yes."

"What are you, then," Alea asked, "to tell the future?"

"Why, she's a seer, of course," Hazel said, "a seer and a Druid."

Alea stared in astonishment. Moira wore only the same loose shirt, loose trousers, and short coat as everybody else, though her jacket was gray, not plaid. Where was the white robe? The sickle at the belt? The wreath of mistletoe?

Where had they been on Versey? Why should a woman Druid dress in the robes of her order any more than a man?

"You've found one of them?" Hazel asked in skeptical amusement. "Where, may I ask?"

"Here," Moira said. "Right here."

"Here? But there's only . . ." Hazel caught her meaning and turned to Alea. *"You?"*

The other Gregors muttered to one another in consternation.

"You're a peace-preacher?" Hazel asked, gawking.

"I'm a healer," Alea said over her sinking heart, "and a trader. Healers hate the fighting that maims people, and, frankly, feuds are bad for the peddler's business. I don't preach peace, but I would find it awfully convenient."

"How long a march is it from wanting peace, to preaching it?" someone asked, scowling.

Alea couldn't tell who it was; they were all scowling now. She turned to them and said, "There's no danger in preaching peace, if the preacher doesn't belong to a clan!"

"There's truth in that," Hazel said grudgingly. "That's half the reason we always welcome Moira, though we know we'll have to endure her cant."

"And the other half?" Alea asked.

"She's a Druid."

It was nice to know the clergy were still honored a little. Alea turned back to Moira. "Perhaps I should become a Druid."

"I'll be glad to teach you," the young woman said, "if I travel with you."

The Gregors turned to exclaim to one another, almost in alarm.

"Peace, friends!" Alea called, smiling. "You'll be passing me on to another clan soon enough. Surely you can't object to escorting both of us for a few more miles." Out of the corner of her eye, she noticed Moira relaxing a little.

The Gregors didn't look convinced.

"Of course, if you really don't want to, we can always go on by ourselves."

"No, we can't have that," Hazel said quickly. "If anything happened to you, our honor would be stained for years." She turned to Moira. "None of your preaching, though, not while we're with you! We're enjoying the journey and we don't want it to become a burden!"

"I'll not talk peace while I'm with you," Moira promised, smiling.

"Then come along." Alea held out a hand. "Tell me what else you foresee."

"The lady was buried in the high chancel,
And the lord, he was buried in the choir.

And out of the lady grew a red rose bush,
And out of the lord a sweet briar.

"They grew till they crept up the walls of the church,
And climbed each side of the spire,
Where they met and twined in a firm love-knot,
For all true lovers to admire!"

Gar nodded his approval. "Very good. A most charming conceit."

"They'd have had a right to feel proud," Kerlew said, "if they'd been alive to see it." He looked around at the trees to either side of the road. "Can't be much of anyone nearby, or they'd have challenged us an hour ago."

"They certainly must have heard us," Gar agreed, "but who would trouble two honest peddlers?"

"There are other outlaws besides Rowena's band," Kerlew told him.

"Why would they want to attack two madmen?"

Kerlew stared at him a moment, then grinned. "Who but a madman would sing at the top of his voice in the forest, eh?"

"Who but a madman would want to attract attention?" Gar returned. "Not that we . . ." He broke off, staring at Kerlew.

Kerlew stared back.

"Ouch," Gar said tentatively.

"Your shin?" Kerlew asked.

"How did you guess?"

"Because mine hurts, too."

As one, they turned and looked down.

A score of people blocked their way—and they needed a score, for they were only two feet tall. The ones right next to the travelers held spears pressed just under the peddlers' knees.

"Who are you," one of them asked in a high, reedy voice, "to go singing so loudly in our woods?"

Gar stared; they were most amazing little people. Each

brandished a spear and held a cocked crossbow too, for they had four arms. They wore kilts and garlands of flowers and leaves, and their heads were covered with fur, not hair, fur that was gray and tawny and orange and brown, but it stopped at forehead and cheeks, leaving eyes, noses, and mouths bare. Their ears were pointed, but high on the sides of their heads. Their button noses were triangular, the mouths lipless, and their eyes had vertical pupils. The resemblance to the fairies Gar had seen was striking, their descent from cats just as clear. "A cousin species," he murmured.

"Cousin? To whom?" the leader demanded.

"To a hawk," said the outlaw. "My name is Kerlew."

The little man gave him a glare that should have bored a hole in his forehead. "Hawks quickly learn to beware of us."

"I have learned it already," Kerlew said with complete sincerity, and bowed. "I honor you, Old One. I would never hunt one of your kind."

"Nor would it do you any good," the little one retorted, "for we are expert at hiding."

"You certainly must be," Gar said, "for you appeared from nowhere."

"And will disappear as quickly, when we have done with you." But the little one was clearly flattered, fairly preening.

"Done with us?" Kerlew's eyes were wide, and a drop of sweat trickled across his brow.

Gar could feel his fear and read the flashes of gruesome scenes from old folktales that flickered through his mind—and Gar noticed that the Wee Folks' spears and arrows may have been tipped with flint and copper, but looked very sharp nonetheless. "Why, what will you do?"

"Let you go your way, if we decide you are unlikely to harm us or the forest," the leader answered. "The first of your kind hunted us down one by one, and chopped down the trees to plant your silly crops!"

So, then. They were a native species who had been solitary, as most cats are, but who had learned to band together to survive in the face of human settlement. "And if you decide we are not?"

The leader didn't answer, only smiled, revealing rows of pointed cat teeth.

Kerlew swallowed thickly. "There are tales. Those who offend the Wee Folk see their cows go dry, their chickens lose their feathers, their hogs go loose to lose themselves in the woods."

"Those are mere punishments," the elf said disdainfully, "warnings that the farmer has offended us, and can yet mend his ways."

"What if he cannot mend his ways?" Gar asked. "Or comes to the forest to hunt?"

The little one dismissed the question with a gesture. "A buck or two we do not mind, if all its meat is eaten. But wholesale slaughter, now, that offends us."

"Or injuring your own kind," Kerlew muttered.

The whole band set up a yowling complaint, and the leader, hissed, "It were better for such a hunter to have died on the horns of his prey!"

Gar could see that half their power was simply the superstitious fear that generations of Wee Folk had built up in the humans, but he was very curious as to the other half. "If you can make cows go dry and chickens lose their feathers, you must be masters of herb lore."

"We are that," the leader snapped, "and can make humans break out in boils and shingles, too!"

"Or worse." Kerlew licked his lips and confided to Gar, "There are tales of people who have fallen in their tracks, then wakened to find they had lost the use of one whole side of the body—or even dropped dead!"

So the Wee Folk had spread rumors exploiting strokes and heart attacks—or could their herbs really have caused them? Gar realized that a whole planetful of alien plants might well have produced chemicals that could maim or kill Earth folk.

But that cut two ways; Terran spices and substances could be lethal to the natives. "That may be true, but you dare not go into a house or barn that is protected by Cold Iron."

Most of the elves hissed and shrank away, but the leader stood its ground and grinned again. "Of course we dare! Cold Iron does not taint the air beneath it, after all."

"Very true," Gar said thoughtfully, "but what happens if it touches you?"

More hissing, and the elves who didn't, spat curses in their own language instead. "We sicken, it is true . . ."

"Or die, if the iron pierces you?"

The band howled and surged forward, spears jabbing upward.

"Peace, peace!" Gar stepped backward quickly. "I only ask! I didn't draw my own blade!"

"Why ask if you know the answer?" the leader demanded.

"I only guess," Gar said. "I don't know. Cold Iron poisons you, doesn't it?"

"As our shards and points poison your kind, when we have dipped them in the blood of the forest!"

Poisoned arrowheads, then, coated with sap or extracts of plants humanity's forebearers never knew.

The elves howled approval, shaking their weapons.

"There is no defense against them," Kerlew said to Gar under cover of the noise. "They shoot tiny darts from hiding that melt in the wounds. No one can ever see their ambush before the point stings."

Gar could believe it; the Wee Folk must have been adept at hiding and at camouflage. "We can always duck."

"Do you truly think so?" The leader grinned, raising its spear. "Try it, mortal man! You shall even see when I throw— much good may it do you!"

"But I don't come to hunt, I come to trade!" Gar dropped to one knee, just in case the elf did hurl the spear, and pulled his pack around as an excuse. He unbuckled the straps, saying, "If you know so much of the powers of the plants, you should have potions that can cure as well as maim! Surely I have some goods that will delight you!"

"Beware!" cried an elf. "What will he draw from that pack?"

"Leave off!" cried a dozen voices, and an elf toward the back raised a crossbow, leveling it at Gar.

"Treachery!" Kerlew leaped in front of Gar, a knife with a foot-long blade appearing in his hand.

Suddenly the air was full of gauzy wings and a crowd of fairies hovered all about them, crying, "Leave the Wee Folk alone!" and hurling tiny objects that winked in the sunlight as they shot toward the outlaw.

Kerlew cried out in horror, twisting and turning aside, but half a dozen of the bright shards buried themselves in his scalp and neck. He fell down as though dead, and a dozen hot needles seemed to pierce Gar's brain. He clutched his head, screaming, "Chop it off! Chop it off to make the pain stop!"

The Gregor party camped in a sort of three-sided cabin, a trail shelter. There wasn't room for the whole party, so half of them spread their blanket rolls on beds of evergreen boughs. Resolved to honor Moira's promise not to preach, Alea asked her, "I'm from very far away, and though I've guested at homesteads, I've heard no stories save those about the feuds. Are there any others?"

"Oh, a host of them!" Moira smiled, dimpling prettily. "Most are told to lull children to sleep, though."

"Well, I'm not sleepy yet." Alea wrapped her arms around her knees and leaned her chin on them. "Tell me one."

"Oh, I suppose my favorite is that of the two sisters who loved the same suitor." Moira settled into the telling of the wicked sister who drowned the good sister, and of the minstrel who found the good sister's breastbone, made a harp of it, and played it at the wicked sister's wedding feast, whereupon the harp sang the truth of the murder.

The clansfolk fell silent as she talked until all were listening. When she finished, one said, "There's not too much of peace-preaching in that."

"There is, if you think about it," Hazel said, frowning.

"Is there?" Moira asked in surprise, then frowned too. "Well, yes, I suppose there is, if you think of war as murder. I only thought of it as a tale of justice winning out, though."

Hazel's frown deepened. "Do you say that peace is justice?"

"Not I," Moira said slowly, "but I think you just have. I'll need to think about that awhile."

A man groaned. "Oh no, Hazel! You've given her fuel for another sermon!"

"Quickly, tell another tale!" Hazel said.

"I know one of a miser who spied on the fairies at their dancing," Alea offered.

An uneasy silence fell. The clansfolk looked at one another, then away, not quite meeting Alea's eyes. "We'd just as soon have no tales of the fairies," Hazel said, "nor of the Wee Folk, either."

"Speaking of them might draw them to us," Moira explained to Alea.

"Oh!" Alea knew enough to respect superstition—and having come from a planet where dwarves and giants were real, she wasn't terribly certain what was superstition and what wasn't. "Then you won't want to hear tales of ghosts, either."

"Oh no, ghosts are perfectly all right," Hazel said, and the clansfolk leaned forward with relish.

Alea managed to shake off her surprise. "Well, then, I'll tell you of a wise teacher who made a man of clay and brought him to life by magic."

Several of the clansfolk shivered with delight, and Hazel said, "Aye! What was the teacher's name?"

"MoHaRaL—well, that was his title," Alea amended, remembering the tale as she had read it on Herkimer's screen. "His people lived surrounded by others who didn't like them, so they never knew when their enemies might attack . . ."

The crowd scowled and muttered, and Alea realized that this sounded far too much like their own lives. She hurried on. "So MoHaRaL went down to the river in the gray light before dawn and sculpted a huge man out of the mud of the bank, and recited magical spells that brought him to life—but since he had no soul, MoHaRaL called him by the word that meant 'incomplete' in his language—'golem.' "

Then she was off, telling them how the golem chopped wood and carried water for everyone on the holy day when they weren't supposed to work, and guarded the homestead at night. "Then the enemies attacked, and the golem fought them off."

The clansfolk were listening, wide-eyed and fascinated now.

"But MoHaRaL found blood on the golem's hands and recited a spell that canceled the first, and the golem fell to the ground, lifeless once more."

The clansfolk burst into cries of indignation.

"What? Killed the poor thing just for doing its duty?"

"How did the magician expect him to guard the homestead without fighting?"

"You can't fight off an attack without bloodying your hands!"

Alea stared at them, completely taken aback.

Hazel pointed a trembling finger at Moira. "It's your doing! One day with you and she turns into a peace-preacher herself!"

"It's only a story," Alea objected.

"Yes, and what's the moral of it?" another clanswoman countered. "That it's wrong to fight back when your clan is attacked!"

"Aye!" said a man indignantly. "What did this magician think the golem was going to do—sing his enemies to sleep?"

"Throw them back over the wall," Alea told him. "Knock them back with his fists! He didn't mean for the golem to kill them!"

"Oh, aye," said another with withering scorn. "How can you fight without killing? People always die in a battle, everyone knows that!"

Desperately, Alea said, "They're much more likely to die when you fight with rifles!"

"And how long would we live if we put down our rifles and the Mahons kept theirs?" Hazel demanded.

"Much longer than you do by fighting, if you take their rifles away!"

The clansfolk fell silent, frowning at one another, uncertain, and Alea felt a glow of success. Even to make them stop to think about it was an achievement!

Only a small one, though. Hazel turned back to her and asked, "How do you get close enough to take away their guns?"

That stopped Alea. She glanced at Moira, but the younger woman could only smile at her with sympathy. She turned back to Hazel and admitted, "I haven't figured that out yet."

"Well, let us know when you do."

"Let me try another story," Alea said quickly. "It's about a gloomy old castle called the Tower of London. Duke Richard sent his nephews there to keep them safe, when his brother the king died. Then he had himself crowned, and no one ever saw the two boys again . . ."

She told them the first of the many tales of the Bloody Tower that she had read on Herkimer's screens and was very relieved that no one saw it as an indictment of Richard III and Henry Tudor, for fighting over the crown. They could have called it a peace-sermon—after all, no matter who won, the little princes lost—but they would have had to stretch.

Instead, the clansfolk seemed to have forgotten reality in place of stories for the moment. Hazel told a tale of a dragon hunter, and Ezra told of the man who saved Death from dying himself, when he'd been beaten sorely by a giant who refused to admit his time had come. The evening passed merrily until Hazel finally stood up and stretched. "While we're waiting, I think I'll sleep. Who wants first watch?"

The mood for storytelling was still with them when they woke up, but it shifted to tall tales. Around the campfire over their morning brew, the clansfolk rivaled to see who could invent the most impossible anecdote.

"So Marl the Smith made a rifle with ten barrels that went around and around as Geordie fired . . ."

"He'd still have to stop to reload *some* time! Besides, what would he hunt with a gun like that? Burley the Hunter, now, he noticed the branches of the trees were broken twenty feet high, but no lower, so he tracked the monster that had done it. Let me tell you, it had hoof-tracks the size of dinner plates . . ."

"So the farther along that pass Brandy went, the more boys there were coming out to follow her, until she brought them out of the gully and they found themselves looking at three packs of wolves, a whole fifty of them, and each one of them as big as a pony . . ."

They kept up the tale-telling even as they broke camp and drowned the fire, so they set off on the road in gusty high spirits that lasted a mile and a half, till they rounded a bend and found a score of clansfolk drawn up three deep across the road, rifles in their hands.

10

The Gregors stopped in their tracks, laughter dying on their lips, rifles rising.

"Good thing you're under a peddler's truce," said the man in the middle of the line. "You Gregors track like bulls blundering through thickets. We heard you half a mile away."

"We must be really bad if a Campbell can hear us," Hazel said with an edge to her voice. "But if we hadn't been escorting a peddler, you may be sure you wouldn't even have guessed we were coming."

The leader's eyes sparked, but before he could dream up an insult, his gaze fell on Moira. He stared; then, affronted, he demanded, "What're you doing back so soon, Moira?"

"Don't worry, Jethro, I'm not," Moira said, amused. "I've only joined this peddler for company on the road."

"And she's going to the Tossians," Hazel snapped, "not to you Campbells."

"Just like a Gregor—trying to tell everyone else what to do."

Alea thought there was something a little weary about the exchange of insults, as though it were a necessary ritual that nobody really enjoyed any more.

"Just like a Campbell, waylaying a peddler who might bypass their clan!"

"Well, as to that, we'd like to ask differently." The clansman took off his hat as he turned to Alea. "We've one took bad sick, miz, and we've heard you're a healer."

Alea glanced left and right and was amazed that none of the Gregors even thought to ask how the Campbells had heard of her so soon. There was a chink in the armor of the clans, perhaps only one sentry calling out boasts to his enemy's watchman, bragging about the healer who had chosen to honor his clan with her presence, and that watchman had told the whole clan, and another sentry had gone out to the far boundary and boasted to a third clan—the Campbells, in this instance.

Which meant they were talking to each other. That talk might be nothing but insults and braggings, but it was communication nonetheless. Alea would have to find out how to use that communication to lighten the feuds, not increase them, that was all.

All! But how? She shelved the question for another day.

"I'll heal whoever is ill," Alea said, then remembered something else from Herkimer's database. "The Oath of Hippocrates demands it."

"Hippocrates?"

"What clan was he from?"

Campbell and Gregor were both instantly suspicious.

"He was the founder of medicine in a land far away," Alea explained, "the first healer. He swore to heal anyone who was ill wherever he found them—stranger or neighbor, rich or poor, enemy or friend."

Clansfolk were nodding slowly; the idea seemed to make sense to them. Healers and Druids, after all, were neutral.

"Well, it's your choice," Hazel said, scowling, "but I hope you don't expect much of Campbell hospitality."

"Don't worry, it will be better than a Gregor could manage," Jethro said with a glare at Hazel, but it didn't have much spirit behind it.

"I don't heal for pay," Alea said, "neither in kind nor in kindness. Simple food and a roof over my head is all I expect." She turned back to Hazel. "Hospitality such as yours is a pleasant bonus."

"Then you'll have an even more pleasant surprise at the Campbell homestead," Jethro averred. "If you'll come with us, lady, you won't regret it."

"If I heal your sick ones, I won't," Alea told him, then to Hazel and her Gregors she said, "Good-bye, then. Thank you very much for good guesting and fine company on the march. I'm sorry to have taken you so far out of your way, but I did enjoy your presence."

"As we enjoyed yours, and the trip together." Hazel smiled and caught her hand. "Thank you for our kinswoman's life, Alea. Our house is yours, whenever you wish it."

"As is ours," Jethro rumbled. "Lady, will you walk with us?"

"That I will," Alea said, and strode away with the Campbells, but she turned back to wave at the Gregors before they were quite out of sight.

"Stop! Stop!" cried a dozen voices, and the elf leader called, "He only sought to protect his friend!"

The pains ceased as suddenly as they had come, and Gar sagged with relief.

"We thought the tall one might be a friend to us, too," one of the fairies trilled, "but what does he seek to bring forth from that pack?"

Gar let go of the twist of paper that held a dozen needles and pulled out a knot of ribbons instead.

"Move slowly," the bird-voice warned.

Gar winced at a reminder, a pain that twisted in his brain and was gone. "Only some pretty things that might delight the Wee Folk," he protested.

"He may indeed be a friend," the lead elf told the fairies. "Certainly he shows a friend's interest."

"A friend's?" asked the fairy. "Or a hunter's?"

The elf shrugged. "We have given him warning, but were only beginning to let him show good will."

"I mean no harm," Gar told them, then frowned. "But I will protect myself as well as I can, and my friend." He stared meaningfully at the fairy and readied a mental bolt of his own.

"Do not fear for the young one," another fairy said contemptuously. "He only sleeps—he is not dead."

"We do not kill lightly," explained another.

"Nor do I," Gar assured them. He frowned from the one group to the other. "But how is this? Do fairies and elves league to protect this wood?"

"We league to protect one another," a fairy said, scowling.

"The New Folk think that we are spirits whom their ancestors feared," an elf explained. "We do all we can to encourage that thought, and punishing their minor crimes, or rewarding their virtues, seems to strengthen it."

"I can see that it would." A dozen stories of elfin capriciousness cascaded through Gar's mind—everything from Rip van Winkle's twenty-year sleep to neat housekeepers finding sixpences in their shoes. "Why only minor crimes, though?"

The elf made a face. "They will not leave off their great sins for any reason. They will murder one another no matter what punishments we visit."

"Because you draw the line at killing them yourself," Gar said slowly.

"Aye, unless they seek to slay us," the elf said darkly. "But for slaughtering one another . . . Well!"

"We will hurt them sorely," a fairy said, "but we will not slay."

"I understand well." Gar had a similar code. Then, daring, he said, "I am greatly honored by your telling me this, but how do you know you can trust me?"

"Oh, we have long ears," the elf said, grinning. "We have heard you speak of seeking to end the continuous havoc these New Folk wreak upon one another."

"I do seek peace," Gar said slowly, "and of course that means peace with your peoples as well as among my own."

"Are they truly yours?" a fairy said pointedly.

Gar felt a chill. "How could they be anything else? Do I not look like them?"

"Save for being taller, aye," the fairy admitted.

"Why then would you think I am not of them?"

"Chiefly because one of our number saw you descend from a golden egg."

Well, Herkimer was more of a discus than an egg, but Gar took the point.

"You and your leman," another fairy added.

"She is not my leman," Gar said automatically, then added in explanation, "only my friend, and my companion in arms."

The fairies exchanged a glance that clearly said they knew his heart better than he did, but they were polite enough not to say it out loud. One turned back to Gar and said, "At least you will not deny that you are both of a kind with the New Folk who war upon one another continually."

"I am of their kind, but not of their nation."

"Not of their nation." An elf nodded. "I like that. But certainly of their kind, for their ancestors, too, did come from the sky."

Gar remembered his earlier encounter with the fairies, and his conjecture that they were native to the planet. "Did not your ancestors also come down from the heavens?"

"They did not," the elf said firmly. "We are of the earth, and our oldest tales tell how the first elves sprang from forest mold."

"And the first fairies from an eagle's aerie," a fairy added.

Gar guessed that they were both right—that the common ancestor of their kind had been a catlike forest creature whose descendants had branched into a tree-living race and an earth-bound race. The first had evolved into a bird's worst nightmare—winged cats—which had evolved further into fairies. The second had evolved into the elves, and the extra two limbs that had been transformed into wings in the fairies had become extra arms in them.

Extra? Surely they only seemed superfluous from a Terran's persepctive! To the elves, he no doubt seeeemed maimed by only having two arms.

"We count you an ally," the fairy said reluctantly, "because you seek peace."

"And, too, because you come well recommended," another fairy chipped in.

The first turned to give her a black look, and Gar found himself wondering who had recommended him—one of the first clansfolk with whom they had stayed? Still, it didn't pay to be too inquisitive, so he asked, "Are you still wary of me?"

"Not at all," an elf said, "for we hear your thoughts, and they are goodly—at least toward us."

Gar froze. Then his brain thawed and kicked into overdrive, a dozen conclusions racing through it in an instant. No wonder both fairies and elves had been able to find him whenever they wanted! No wonder they knew he had come in a spaceship, and no wonder they were sure of his good intentions. They were telepaths!

There was also the matter of his relationship with Alea, but he shoved that issue aside quickly. "You do not hesitate to read people's minds, then, do you?"

"Why should we?" a fairy asked. "All your kind are like open books to us. Wherefore not read?"

"Do you think we break some sort of trust, fellow?" an elf asked, and laughed.

"The New Folk trust us not at all," another elf explained, "nor should they."

"As we should not trust them," a fairy added. "If it were not for the fear we have inspired in them, I doubt not that they would shoot us out of the air for sport."

"We would shoot back well enough." An elf caressed his crossbow.

"Aye, if you could take aim while dodging their boots," a fairy retorted.

Gar sensed that an old, old rivalry had surfaced. To shove it back under, he asked, "Can you not trust some New Folk simply by the good will you read in them?"

"We have done so now and again," a fairy hummed. "We have become keen judges of character."

Gar knew he shouldn't, but couldn't resist. "What is there about my character that lets you trust me, then?"

"Why, we have told you," a fairy replied.

"No, you have told me of my circumstances—descending from a spaceship—and of my intentions, which are to forge a peace," Gar corrected. "Have I no defects of character that make you mistrust me?"

He was astounded when the whole assemblage burst into laughter. He waited it out, somewhat numb, trying not to be resentful. As they quieted, he said sardonically, "I am glad I serve as such a source of mirth."

"No, you are not, and you are highly indignant," an elf said, "as indeed you should be."

"We all can see your defects, New Man," a fairy said, wiping tears from its eyes, "but they are not such as to lessen our trust in you."

"Indeed!" Gar tried to quell his indignation. "May I ask what my defects are, then?"

"A dangerous question," a fairy warned. "No matter how we answer, you will take offense."

"I shall not, by my hand!" Gar held up a palm as though taking an oath.

"Well sworn." An elf nodded approval. "But there is no creature who can fail to take offense when told his defects."

"Why then, I shall strive to remember that I brought it upon myself." Gar felt inspiration strike. "After all, you may have been adding me to the believers in your supernatural abilities, and your unwilling dupe in carrying them to the clans. You have not yet told me anything that you could not have learned by observation, and by a certain empathy born of centuries of watching my kind."

"Oho! It's proof you want, then, is it?" an elf hooted. "Learn, then, New Man, that we know you for the coward you are!"

"I am not a coward!"

"A coward of the heart," a fairy explained, "and with good reason—for five women broke your trust and mangled your feelings."

"Yet those five women were all one," an elf amended. "One in various guises—and skilled indeed she was at disguising."

Gar felt a chill run through him. How could these creatures have peered so deeply into his memories so quickly?

But it hadn't been quickly, of course. They had been tracking him for days, no doubt studying him in depth as he went.

Nevertheless, how could they have discovered that all five women—the ugliest witch in the north country, the wild fey girl, and all the others—had been only one emotional assassin in several disguises? He hadn't known that himself until . . .

Until Gregory had told him the other night. The fairies no doubt had eavesdropped on that conversation.

Anger surged in him; he held himself rigid, waiting for it to pass. What right had these strangers to inspect his most intimate thoughts? Had they no ethics, no standards of telepathy?

No, of course not. They were faced with aliens much larger than themselves, and very violent in the bargain. They felt no compunction in using whatever weapons they had.

They were tense now, elves with crossbows raised, fairies with hands cupped (for what? telepathic beams?), knowing his anger, braced for his wrath—but as the rage began to subside, the Wee Folk began to relax.

"You are angry," one said.

They still held their crossbows at the ready.

"Even as you said," Gar answered in a level tone, "none can hear their detractions without resenting them."

"True," said a fairy "but it is not that which angers you—it is our invasion of what you perceive to be your privacy."

"Even so." Gar bent his head in acknowledgment. "It is a

primitive reflex—but I asked for it. After all, how can I mend my faults if I do not know them?"

"He swallows the bitter pill," an elf said, staring.

"He does indeed," agreed a fairy. "It sticks in his craw, but he swallows it down."

They were all gazing at him in surprise, almost in awe, and Gar realized they had been testing him. Anger boiled up again, but he stood still, waiting for it to crest and subside. If he had passed the test once, he wasn't about to fail it now!

The Wee Folk had tensed again, reading his anger, but as it began to recede once more, they relaxed a little and stared at him with more awe than ever.

"Never have I seen self-control so thorough among one of the New Folk," said a fairy.

"Aye, the more amazing because it stems from his beliefs of what is right and wrong," an elf answered. She made a swirling motion with her hand, saying, "Yet how will he fare when he must stare his fears in the eye?"

The air seemed to thicken into a fog, out of which came the cry, "A rag, a bone!"

A chill coursed through Gar. He knew that voice.

The fog condensed further into a body, one that took on colors—and Gar found himself staring at a portly man dressed like the driver of a Victorian hackney cab in a threadbare caped coat, dented top hat, patched trousers, and Wellington boots, his nose and cheeks ruddy with the tiny broken veins of the chronic drinker, who gave Gar a boozy, cheerful grin. "What of your heart, ardent lover?" the apparition demanded. "Do you hear it knocking to leap free of its golden box yet?"

Superstitious fear seized Gar, though he knew the man for nothing but a projection of his own deepest drives. It wasn't his heart that heaved against its restraints, but his anger, anger that built and built into rage as he realized that the elves had conjured the rag-and-bone man out of the recesses of Gar's mind to test him. He trembled with the strength of the emotion but controlled it with an iron will, saying in a hard level tone, "It has not, praise Heaven! My heart lies quietly, content to rest in security."

"You lie to yourself." The ragpicker waved a finger. "You long to have it out of its prison, to be able to love again."

"Love is a dream," Gar said, his voice still level. "It will come when it comes—but when it does, my heart will swell till it bursts the lock of its own accord."

"There is no breaking that lock," the ragpicker jeered. "Only one with a key can open it."

"Then I am forever safe, for you kept the key," Gar said with a sardonic smile.

"Did I say I kept it?" the ragpicker asked with feigned surprise. "Dear me! If I did, why, I lied—for there is no key!"

There was no surge of anger, only a wave of relief, and Gar was appalled, but he took advantage of the surprise and smiled. "Then I shall wait for a woman with a lock-pick, devious creature, or for one who can forge me a key."

"Then you shall wait all your life," the ragpicker warned.

"So be it," Gar said. "It will be worth the wait."

"Worth it how? Passing your time flitting about the galaxy freeing nations of thankless people? Finishing alone in your old age? Will this make the wait worthwhile?"

"If a woman comes with a key, she will be worth it. If not?" Gar shrugged. "I may not have a gamesome spirit, but I can find many tasks that will amuse me. My life will not be wasted and at its end, I doubt not I will thank you."

"So he speaks to the deepest part of himself," the ragpicker said to the elves with deep disappointment. "Worse, he thinks he means it." He turned back to Gar, shaking his head. "He will not rise to the bait."

"What? To rant and rave at a figment of my own dream-mind?" Gar gave him a thin smile. "That would be a waste of breath indeed."

"It is not that purpose to which I would make you rise," said the ragpicker, but shook his head at the elves. "Let me go, mind-makers. I can be of no use here."

"As you wish it." The elf held her hand up flat, moved it in a circle, and the ragpicker disappeared like steaming breath wiped from a cold window pane.

"We can trust him," the elf said to the fairy. Then her tone took on a note of regret as she added, "Though he cannot trust himself."

"I trust myself to keep my temper no matter what the temptation," Gar said with a smile.

"Aye, more's the pity," a fairy answered, "but can you trust yourself to do what is best for you?"

"Best for me?" Gar asked with another sardonic smile. "Why bother? All my worth comes from making the world better for other people."

"Do you deserve nothing for yourself?"

Gar frowned, thinking it over, then said, "It's not a question of deserving. Making the world a better place makes my life worth living, that's all."

"Should you not also make it a better place for yourself?"

"What would such self-indulgence accomplish?"

"Perhaps a little more happiness."

"Happiness?" Gar smiled. "Yes, I remember that from my childhood." He shrugged. "It will come if it will come."

"Do you not think you merit it?"

Again, Gar shrugged. "If I do, it will find me some day."

The fairy stared at him, eyes wide and tragic, then turned to the elves. "Can we mend him in that?"

"No," said an elf, "nor can his own kind, not even a woman. He can only mend himself."

"And he will not bother." The fairy turned back to Gar. "Nonetheless, we can wish you well in your peace-seeking, wanderer, and will give you whatever aid we can."

"Aye," said an elf. "If ever you are in danger, flee to any of the Keepers of the Mounds and they will give you sanctuary such that no mortal will dare violate."

"I thank you." Gar wondered what the Keepers of the

Mounds were but thought it best not to ask; they would probably be self-evident.

"You are welcome, so long as your enemy is our enemy."

Gar frowned. "But I am of the New People! Are *they* not your enemies?"

"No," said a fairy, "they are only a hazard of which we must be wary."

"It is their warring that hurts us, for when many clansfolk go blasting leaden balls from rifles made of Cold Iron, elves and fairies alike are injured or slain."

"Even the concussion of their firearms can maim us," another fairy said.

Gar looked at the gossamer-winged, fine-boned body and found he could believe it easily. "So, then, we do have a common enemy—the feuds."

"Even so," the fairy agreed. "Labor to end them, mortal, and you shall have the thanks of all the Old People! Farewell."

Wing beats exploded, and the fairies were gone so quickly that if Gar had blinked, he would have thought they had simply disappeared.

"Farewell indeed," an elf seconded, "and be sure that so long as you work for peace, you shall have the aid of the Wee Folk. Good fortune attend you."

"Good fortune," the elves chorused. Then each stepped behind a leaf or tree or sank down into underbrush, and were gone from view as though they had never been.

Gar stared, then opened his mind cautiously and felt the presence of a score of other minds so alien he could scarcely distinguish any of their thoughts. "Au revoir," he said softly, then turned to waken Kerlew, thinking all the while that he would have to work at deciphering the thoughts of the Old Folk until it could become automatic.

He shook the lad's shoulder and Kerlew groaned, but it was only the sort of groan issuing from anyone who sleeps deeply and is reluctant to waken. "Rise, bold woodsman," Gar said softly, "and hunt the sun, or it will be up and away before you can catch it."

The boy rolled over to squint up at Gar, frowning. "What nonsense is this? Who could hunt the sun—and why should he? It will come to us all sooner or later."

"It will indeed," Gar agreed, "and you'll want to be awake to see it. Come now, rise and take some breakfast, for we've a long day's journey ahead."

Kerlew levered himself up, then put a hand to his head, puzzled. "I seem to have slept well . . ." He looked up at Gar. "If sunrise is nearly upon us, then you must have watched all night by yourself! Why did you not wake me for my turn?"

"I was preoccupied." Gar took a quick inventory of his body and said with surprise, "I'm not tired, though. I suppose I will be halfway through the morning. Then I'll trouble you to keep watch while I nap."

"Surely, but I would gladly have done so last . . ." Kerlew's eyes widened as memory caught up with him. "The Wee Folk! We came upon them last night, and they felled me!"

"So they did," Gar agreed, "though they assured me you would only sleep very deeply and were not hurt in any way."

"No wonder you did not wake me." Kerlew looked up at Gar anxiously. "Did they keep you talking all night?"

"I suppose they did," Gar said with surprise, "though it seemed to be less than an hour."

"That is their way." Kerlew rose, dusting himself off. "They can make an instant seem to be a day, or a day pass in an instant. Come, let's breakfast, and we can tell each other what we know of them while we walk."

Over journey rations and a hot herbal brew, Kerlew explained that the clans called the elves the Wee Folk or the Old Ones. "Legend has it that they were on this world when our ancestors came from the stars," he said with a sardonic smile, "but who could believe such an old wives' tale?"

"Who indeed?" Gar reflected wryly that fairies and elves were quite real to the clansfolk, but space travel was a fantasy. "It was rather difficult to know to whom I was talking. I can accept that they all look alike to us, but I couldn't even tell males from females."

"None can," Kerlew told him. "Indeed, no one is even certain that there are two sexes."

"They aren't that different from us, surely!" Gar couldn't be certain, but the natives did look rather mammalian, though he hadn't seen any mammaries. "How else would they reproduce?"

Kerlew spread his hands. "None knows. Some think they may lay eggs, others that they split in half so that each half grows into a new being."

"Now that I would call a fairy tale." Gar knew that fission only worked on the microscopic level.

Kerlew shrugged. "Others guess that elves are male and fairies female, but few place much faith in the notion. The elves are too much larger than the fairies."

"Well, male or female, it matters not," Gar said. "All that matters is that they've said they'll help us, if we seek to bring peace to the clans."

"That can never happen!" Kerlew exclaimed wide-eyed, then immediately corrected himself. "Though mayhap, with the help of the Old Ones . . ." His eyes filled with longing. "It would be pleasant to be able to go home again."

If he did, Gar thought, he would go as a hero, hailed as one of the peacemakers—the very crime for which he had been exiled. He drank the dregs of his tea and stood, kicking dirt on the campfire. "Then let's go find a way to make it happen."

Kerlew rose, too. "Which way lies peace?"

"Everywhere and nowhere." Gar tucked the camping gear back in his pack. "It might lie down any road, so the direction doesn't matter, only the journey."

They left their campsite in considerably better spirits than they had come to it and set off down the road singing. After all, anyone really wanting to ambush travelers would have set sentries on the trackway, so what did it matter if they made some noise?

The argument seemed to lose its logic when the roadside leaves parted and half a dozen people stepped out into the road before them, rifles leveled.

11

C an you cure them, lady?" the grandmother asked in a frosty tone. That, plus the sharp anxiety in her eyes, told Alea how hard she was working to maintain her dignity when she was frightened for her children and grandchildren.

A dozen of the adults and children had sores on their faces and hands. Alea studied the slack-jawed faces of the adults, then asked one woman, "Do your gums bleed?"

"How did you know?" The woman stared at her in amazement, and the others muttered to one another incredulously.

"It's part of this disease," Alea explained. "Have your teeth grown loose?"

"She's a witch!" a man hissed, shaken.

"No, only a healer." Alea turned to the grandmother. "It's nothing to fret about, Lady Grandmother. They're not eating right, that's all."

"Not eating right!" the old woman exploded. "I see to it they've plenty! Cornbread, beans, and molasses, just as their parents and grandparents had!"

"If they did, you must have seen this sickness before," Alea said, and from the haunted look in the grandmother's eyes knew she had guessed rightly. "What kinds of fruits do you grow?"

"Why, apples and pears, like every other clan!"

"No oranges or lemons?"

The grandmother frowned. "What are those?"

Alea guessed the climate was too cold for citrus fruit. "What vegetables, then? Do you grow tomatoes?"

"Aye, for a bit of garnish." The old woman made a face. "Who would want them for anything more?"

"Like them or not, you'd better serve them with the noon meal and the evening meal every day from now on," Alea told her, "and make sure the young ones finish theirs, too."

The old woman frowned. "Will that heal them?"

"Oh, yes," Alea said. "You'll see some improvement in a matter of days, but it will be a month or two before all the symptoms are gone."

"Tomatoes!" The old woman made it sound like an obscenity, then sighed. "Well, you don't bring in a healer to ignore her advice. We'll try it for a fortnight, at least." She turned to one of the younger men. "Jonathan, till a bed and plant more of the blasted things."

"As you will, Grandmother." The boy made a face on his way to the door. Apparently he shared her opinion of tomatoes.

"Now then, Moira." Grandma turned to the seer, one problem disposed of and out of her mind, another problem before her. "Not that you're not welcome, mind you, but how is it you've come back so soon?"

"By the good graces of this healer, Grandma." Moira smiled, amusement showing for a second before she throttled it into bland politeness. "She is graciously allowing me to attend her as a traveling companion."

"Graciously, is it?" Grandma gave Alea a suspicious look, as though tolerating Moira's company automatically made her suspect, but she admitted, "It is better for young women to travel together, though. A solitary road is a long one—and dangerous."

"We trust that even bandits will not assault a healer, Grandma," Alea said demurely.

"Trust no one, when you're on the road," Grandma retorted. "Still, Alea, I find it hard to believe you can tolerate this young preacher's cant."

"We do talk of peace," Alea admitted, "but I don't find it burdensome. I, too, would like to see all the clans put the past behind them and live in harmony. I suppose every healer would, though."

Grandma frowned. "Why, how is that?"

"Why, because we spend so much effort in trying to mend wounds and save lives," Alea said, surprised. "How could we delight in feuds that undo all our work and kill more?"

Grandma pursed her lips, mulling it over. "Hadn't thought of it that way."

"It makes you wonder if there's any point to your work when you see it all undone," Alea told her. "Yesterday I saved a young woman who had just given birth and was bleeding her life away. Two years from now, I might come this way again and find she's been killed in battle. Why then did I go to all the labor of saving her life?"

"Why, to give her two more years," Grandma said, "and her clan another rifle to help defend them." But her expression was dubious.

"What of her baby, then?" Alea said. "I've served as a midwife often enough. What good was helping a baby be born if I come by fifteen years later and see him cut down in a firefight?"

Grandma winced at that one. "Aye, and what point in the months of waddling about with a great weight before you, and of the pain of birthing, and the years of toil and patience and throttling down anger and nurturing, when the little ones are killed before they've scarcely had a chance to live?" She gave herself a shake. "But like it or not, it's the way life is, child. We can't change it, and must try to fare through it as best we may."

"Must we?" Moira said, suddenly intense.

Grandma turned to her glaring, and Alea said quickly, "Maybe we can't change it, Grandma, but we have to try anyway."

Grandma turned back to her. "What point, if you can't succeed? It's wasted labor." Then she caught the echo of her own words and looked uncertain.

"Aye," Alea said softly, "and it's wasted labor trying to save people's lives and heal their wounds. It's a question of which labor I'm willing to waste, Grandma, that's all."

"Well, then, if you think that, why try at all?"

"Because I'm alive," Alea said simply, "and to stop trying is to stop living."

"There's some truth in that," Grandma said grudgingly. "All right, let's say you're going to try to stop the fighting. How would you go about it?"

"Why . . ." Alea stared in surprise, then recovered and answered, "The same way I go about healing—find the cause, then seek the remedy."

"Well, that makes sense," Grandma allowed. "You can't fix something if you don't know how it broke. But what causes a feud, child?"

"I'll have to ask you that," Alea said gently. "What started your feud with the Gregors?"

"Started it?" Grandma asked, as though surprised that anyone wouldn't know. "Why, Colum Gregor shot Great Uncle Hiram in the woods when Hiram was only out hunting, not doing anybody a lick of harm!"

"Going about peaceful work, not bothering anybody?" Alea frowned. "Why did Colum shoot him, then?"

"Because he was a wicked one and a villain, that's why!"

"And a low-down, sneaky, treacherous snake, too," said one of the clansmen, coming near. "Shot Uncle Hiram in the back, he did."

"Those Gregors are all backstabbers," said a middle-aged woman, coming forward in indignation. "They'd kill you as soon as look at you, and steal your daughters into the bargain."

"Oh." Alea looked up. "So Colum had stolen Hiram's daughter, then?"

"No, it was young Malcolm stole my daughter Sairy!" the woman exclaimed. "Stole her away in the dead of night, he did, and right from out the midst of her kinfolk, too!"

"Laid a ladder against the side of the house and climbed up bold as brass to knock her on the head and carry her off," another woman added.

"Slipped past the sentries and drugged the dogs," the clansman said, glowering.

But Alea saw a teenaged girl sitting by the hearth staring rigidly into the fire, her fists clenched, and knew there was more to the story. "How do you know he knocked her on the head?"

"Know!" cried the mother. "Why, I daresay she wouldn't have gone with him any other way, now would she?"

It sounded like quite a feat to Alea—impossible, in fact. "And his kinfolk applauded him for this?"

"Applauded?" the woman cried, scandalized. "Not even a Gregor would let a man stay if he consorted with the enemy! No, they cast him out, right enough."

"Then Sairy came back to you?"

"How could she, when she'd been with an enemy man?" the clansman demanded. "No, she was outcast too, of course."

For a moment, sorrow threatened to overwhelm the mother, but she forced it back, squaring her shoulders and holding her head high.

Alea watched the teenager in front of the fire out of the corner of her eye; the girl was biting her lip and fighting back tears. She changed the subject. "Was that the first time a Gregor man had courted a Campbell woman?"

An uneasy silence fell, and the clansfolk glanced at one another. Then Grandma lifted her chin and said, "That was the third time."

"When was the first?"

"Why, when Colum and Hiram both courted Esther Avenell, that's when!"

"I see," Alea said slowly. "And she married Colum?"

"That she did, the worthless trollop! That's why Hiram went hunting—to be off by himself and alone with his grief."

"At least he gave a good account of himself," the clansman grunted. "His shot broke Colum's shoulder. A little lower and he would have killed his killer."

Or was it Colum who had died defending himself? Alea wondered if Hiram had tried to ambush Colum but found the Gregor a little faster than himself, a little more accurate. Certainly that would be the way the Gregors told it.

She felt very sorry for Esther Avenell Campbell, to be the cause of so much bloodshed and the beginning of a feud, but she felt glad for her, too, because she had married for love, from the sound of it, and her husband had lived. "I don't suppose it could have been a hunting accident."

"I suppose not indeed!" Sairy's mother said indignantly.

"But it wouldn't matter if it had been." Grandma leaned forward, locking gazes with Alea. "If one of your clan is slain, you have to take revenge, child. Otherwise there's nothing to keep anyone from slaying every one of your kith and kin out of malice alone."

"You speak of revenge," Alea said. "What of justice?"

"Justice?" Grandma made the word a mockery. "Who's going to give us justice, child? Who could we trust to see the truth and render judgment? Where could we find someone who wasn't partial to the one clan or the other?"

And that, Alea realized, was the nub of the problem. With no impartial judge, no code of laws, no peace officers, there was no way to seek redress and be satisfied the dead had been fairly treated—or that the living would be protected.

"Great Uncle Hiram you called him," Alea said to Grandma. "He was your father's brother, then?"

"Heavens, no, child!" Grandma said. "More like a great-great-great-great-great . . . well, you get the idea."

Sairy's mother intervened. "This was ages and ages ago, Lady Healer—three hundred years and more."

Alea stared at her, dumbstruck. For three centuries, clansmen had been killing each other over something that might have been a hunting accident or their own ancestor's crime. "Three hundred years!" she gasped. "Hasn't that crime grown cold yet? Can it still matter to you that Hiram was killed?"

"Yes it can!" the clansman said.

"But even if it didn't, the death of two of my five sons does." Grandma leaned forward, trying to make Alea understand. "It's not the deaths that happened a hundred years ago that matter to us, child—it's the ones that happened twenty years ago, and ten, and last year, and last month! It's the wounds that our living kinfolk bear, the suffering they've lived through! It's David's limp and the pain his leg gives him whenever the weather gets damp; it's Jael's stump of an arm and the way she weeps whenever it thunders." She leaned back, chin high. "Oh, yes, child, the past matters—the past and the present."

"And the future," Sairy's mother said. "If we don't take revenge for those who have died, those Gregors will feel free to kill off every last one of our children!"

"Can't you see that the fighting is a greater danger still?" Moira burst out. "Can't you see that your only chance for a long and happy life is peace?"

All the clansfolk turned frosty eyes to her. "No, we can't see that, peace-lover." The clansman made the word an obscenity. "We can't believe in peace, for who'd see to it that it was just and lasting?"

"You're right in this," a woman told Alea, "that it doesn't really matter any more whether Colum shot first, or Hiram did. There's been too much blood shed since, too great a need for vengeance grown."

"Aye," said Sairy's mother. "What do I care about some woman who lost her man fifty years ago? I care about my man that those Gregors killed when he wasn't but twenty-six, and us married only eight years with five kids!"

"The past may be dead, Lady Healer," said Grandma, "but the anger that it brought still lives."

• • •

The clansfolk weren't rude enough to let their anger make them turn guests away from the table, but Alea sensed that they needed some time to cool off, so she told one of the women that she and Moira would gather herbs until suppertime. The woman seemed glad to hear it, so the seer and the healer went out to hunt rue and rosemary.

They passed the barn and both women stopped, falling silent in respect as they saw the teenaged girl huddled on a bale by the corner, weeping quietly. She had escaped from her place by the fire and could let the tears fall. Alea and Moira exchanged a glance, then moved up to her. "Come now, lass," Alea said gently, "it can't be as bad as that."

The girl looked up, startled, then blotted her face furiously with her apron. "Can't a body have a quiet cry now and then? Isn't there any place I can be alone?"

"Not that you can be sure of, from what your kinfolk were saying." Moira knelt, holding out her hands. "Come now, I'm Moira, and this is Alea, and at least we feel as sorry for Malcolm and Sairy as you do."

The girl stared. "How did you know I was weeping for them?"

"Because we could see through the nasty things people were saying about them." Alea sat beside her. "Who are you?"

"Cicely," the girl said, almost automatically. "How come you don't believe what they said about Malcolm and Sairy?"

"You don't really think one man alone could gag a woman, tie her up, and carry her struggling down a ladder by himself, do you?" Alea asked.

"Not without knocking over the ladder," Moira said, "and his kinsmen certainly wouldn't have helped him, since marriage with the enemy is forbidden."

"They didn't." Cicely looked down at her lap, plucking at her apron. "It was just Malcolm alone, that's certain."

"I thought as much," Alea said. "But they're away and happy now, so why do you care so deeply what your kinsfolk say about them?"

"Why, because they're making Sairy sound like a hussy and a traitor," Cicely burst out, "and she's not, she's sweet and pure and good! She couldn't help it if she fell in love with a Gregor, she couldn't!"

"No, of course she couldn't," Alea soothed. "Where did they meet, then?"

"Down by the stream. Sairy told me that she went to drink where he was standing sentry-go on the bank across from her, but they saw each other and leveled their rifles and shouted at the same moment. Then they stared at each other and both burst out laughing. When they stopped, they both looked at each other and felt something magical happen."

"So that's how it began," Moira said softly. "And they kept meeting there?"

"There, or wherever they'd been told to stand guard," Cicely said. "They'd each volunteer for the night watch and the worst place, the gully where it's so harsh and lonely, just to be near enough to talk."

"And after a while, they started wanting something more than talk?"

"They never did more than kiss!" Cicely said fiercely. "He swam a nighttime river to hold her in his arms, and finally they couldn't keep from it any more and kissed, but that's all!"

"I'm sure." Alea thought of the consequences of having a baby out of wedlock in this culture and shivered. "But they did decide to run away together."

"Well . . . yes," Cicely admitted. "But that's not . . . you know . . ."

"They're going to find a Druid first," Moira filled in for her. "After she marries them properly, what they do is nobody's concern but their own."

Cicely eyed her suspiciously. "How'd you know our Druid's a woman, Moira?"

The seer smiled. "You forget how long I've been tramping this countryside trying to persuade folks to listen to reason, Cicely. I know every clan and outlaw band—so a strange seer

I'd be if I didn't know the Druids, too. How did they really run away?"

"Why, down a ladder from her bedroom window, just as they told you," Cicely said in surprise. "Malcolm left it there, after all. He wasn't about to carry it with them."

"But Sairy climbed down of her own free will?" Alea asked.

"Free and eager." Cicely nodded emphatically. "Scared of what they were doing, but eager to be with Malcolm for good."

"How did Malcolm manage to slip past the sentries and silence the dogs?"

"Why, because Sairy told him where the sentries were stationed and what time their relief would come," Cicely said. "He knew to creep through the woods during the last hour of their watch."

"When they would be most sleepy." Alea nodded. "What about the dogs?"

"Sairy mixed the sleeping potion in their food that night."

"So it wasn't an abduction, but an elopement." Alea smiled. "I wondered how Malcolm managed all that by himself."

"You won't tell on me, will you?" Cicely asked anxiously.

"Of course not." Privately, Alea didn't think there was much to tell—they couldn't have been the only ones who had noticed her grief. "But you've given us another reason for wanting to bring peace."

"Why's that?" Cicely asked, wide-eyed.

"So Sairy can come home," Alea said, "if only to visit."

"They'd never have her!" Cicely exclaimed. "She's their shame and their horror!"

"I think a mother's love is stronger than that," Moira said with gentle sympathy. "She works hard at not showing it, but Sairy's mother is grieving even more deeply than you."

"Do you really think so?" Cicely asked.

"Yes, I do," Moira said, "and if we meet Sairy on our travels, I'll tell *her* that I think so, too."

"Meet Sairy! Oh, miss!" Cicely clasped Moira's hands. "If you do, you'll come back and tell me how she fares, won't you?"

"Yes, we will," Moira assured her. "Come, now, and help us seek herbs."

"No, I dasn't." Cicely stood with an anxious glance at the sun. "My heavens! Is it that late? They'll skin me alive if I'm not back in time for my watch."

"Go, then," Alea said with a smile, "but try not to feel badly if they speak against Sairy again."

"I won't, if I can think of you finding and talking to her. Thank you, ladies, thank you!" Then Cicely hurried back to the house.

"That helped her a little," Moira said as they went on toward the woods.

Alea nodded. "I'm glad we could cheer her that much, at least. What do you suppose was the truth about Hiram's killing?"

"That Colum tracked him through the woods, caught him when he was alone, and shouted some insult before he fired," Moira said. "The more fool he, giving his victim a chance to turn and shoot."

"Hiram must have been very quick and very accurate," Alea said doubtfully.

"Have you seen my people shoot?" Moira asked. "When they hunt pheasants, they shoot for the head, so as not to have to worry about lead in their dinners."

Alea shuddered. "Do they always hit their marks?"

"More often than not," Moira answered, "and a man's a much bigger target than a bird. But as to Hiram's speed, well, I'll admit he'd have to have been keyed up, on edge, to be able to spin about so quickly. I wonder what he was hunting—a bear?"

"Or Colum?" Alea asked grimly. "You don't suppose she encouraged them both, do you?"

"Not as far as engagement, no," Moira said. "Of course, that wouldn't have mattered to some men. They'd think they should have whatever they wanted—and if she were a true beauty, one look at her would be enough to make Colum love her."

Personally, Alea didn't think any of the clanswomen were

terribly attractive, but she asked herself who she was to judge and resolved to ask Gar when she found him. "So you don't think Colum was really in love with her."

"Only in the way that a man's in love with his rifle or anything else he owns," Moira said. "If he'd really loved her, he'd have wanted her to be happy, wouldn't he?"

"So he wouldn't have tried to kill her fiancé. Yes." Alea lifted her head and sighed. "I always thought it would be romantic to have men fighting over me, that it would make me feel important, desired. But it doesn't, does it?"

"Doesn't and isn't," Moira said, and the dryness of her tone made Alea wonder if she knew from personal experience.

Why had Moira started wandering, anyway?

For all her bulk, Evanescent the alien could move as silently as a zephyr when she chose. Nonetheless, she knew dozens of eyes watched her as she prowled the woods, for she could hear the thoughts behind them. She smiled with complacency at the consternation of the fairies and elves, alarmed because they couldn't hear her thoughts. Well, they would soon enough, when she found a place to make her stand.

There! A huge boulder jutted from the soil, slant-sided and flat-topped. Evanescent padded up its side and sat at the summit, looking down a dozen feet at the forest below her. It was a decent podium; it would do. She unleashed a thought at the Old Ones.

Panic, anger, and horror swept through the clearing.

Evanescent frowned and spoke aloud. "Come now! If I'd wanted to hurt you, I'd have done it. Why not come forth to parley with me? I won't eat you, I swear it."

"Try, and you'll choke on your meal," said a grim and buzzing voice.

12

An elf rose from the mold of the forest floor, fists clenched, glaring straight into Evanescent's eyes.

"There now!" the alien said with a smile. She kept her lips closed and her shark-teeth hidden, though. "Am I so horrible as all that?"

"You're large," the elf temporized.

"You can tell your friend behind that bush that his dart is far too small to pierce my fur." It wasn't, but Evanescent had to take a chance somewhere, didn't she? "And your colleague on the tree limb above me will find my ear a far smaller target than she thinks."

"We know where you are, too, you know," a counter tenor called down to her.

"Of course," Evanescent said. "I'm right out here where you can see me. Why don't you step out, too?"

"There really isn't much point in cover, when she can tell our whereabouts by our thoughts," a bell-like voice admitted.

"No, and it will give us better aim," the first elf pointed out.

"Enough, then! Out one and all!"

They were there so suddenly that even Evanescent missed

seeing them step out from behind trunks and stones, leaves and bushes. A dozen fairies hovered six feet over her head, just beneath the lowest branches, each with a slender bow bent and an arrow nocked. Elves clustered below her on the forest floor or sat on the limbs above, each with a crossbow and spear leveled at her.

"That's better, now," Evanescent purred. "We can talk as spirits should."

"Spirit!" said an elf with a laugh. "You're no more a spirit than we are!"

"No less either, though," Evanescent pointed out, "and the New Folk don't know we're only flesh and blood, like them."

"New Folk yourself!" cried a fairy. "We saw you climb down that golden ramp!"

"I only meant to hide from the ship itself," Evanescent protested, "and from its passengers, of course."

"Of course?" asked an elf. "They don't know about you, then?"

"I try to be certain they don't," the alien answered.

"But they're yours clear as spring water," a fairy retorted. "Don't try to say they're not."

"Well, I don't own them."

"And don't run them, either, I suppose," an elf said with sarcasm.

"No, that I don't," Evanescent said primly. "I only watch their antics and do the best I can to let them keep on."

" 'The best you can?' " Another elf scowled. "You mean you help them?"

"Once I understand what they're trying to do, yes," Evanescent answered. "After all, they only have the good of their own silly kind of people at heart."

"But not the good of ours," a fairy snapped.

"That's so." Evanescent looked up at her. "Though there are some matters that benefit all people, Old and New alike."

"Such as?" an elf challenged.

"Peace," Evanescent answered.

Peace there was, or silence at least, while elves and fairies alike digested the fact that this strange creature wanted peace, too.

Then an elf said, "Your pet male claims to be trying to bring peace to all the clans."

"He's his own man," Evanescent protested, "or at least not mine. Bringing peace is his idea, but I think it will be very amusing to watch him try."

"Then your pleasure is apt to be short-lived," an elf said darkly. "These New Folk tend to take a dim view of peacemakers."

"Yes, well, that's why I'm doing what I can to keep him alive," Evanescent said, "and why I'm going to ask you to do the same."

"Us protect him?" a fairy demanded. "Why should we?"

"Because peace would be good for us as well as the New Folk," an elf answered. "One of our troops has already promised him aid in it."

"You don't think he really can make them stop shooting one another, do you?" the fairy asked.

"Who knows?" The elf shrugged. "Why not let him try? After all, he might succeed."

"Even if he doesn't, it's delightful watching him," Evanescent told them.

"You've a strange idea of fun." The elf looked at her with a jaundiced eye. "Remind me not to play with you."

"I wouldn't dream of it," Evanescent assured him. "I let others do my playing for me."

"Lazy wight, aren't you?" a fairy said with scorn.

"I earn my pleasure," Evanescent told her, "earn it by helping my toys play their games—and the longer they live, the longer they keep away boredom for me. That gives me reason to help them while I can."

"I suppose we will, too," a fairy said grudgingly. "You'll want us to protect your female, too, of course."

"Chances are double with two working," Evanescent replied.

"Of course," the elf said with a withering look. "Any other

little thing you'd like to ask of us? Shall we move a mountain for you? Make a river flow upstream?"

"Don't tell them you've seen me, of course," Evanescent answered, "let alone talked to me."

The elf gave her a long, narrow look. "Somehow I don't think I'll want to admit that, to them or any of the New Folk. All right, creature, we'll aid them and you'll aid them, and perhaps somehow they'll bring peace to this sick and death-loving people."

"Of course," Evanescent agreed. "After all, we spirits must stick together."

Leaves rustled behind them, and Gar knew there were more hard-faced people in floppy hats, loose trousers, and oversized jackets stepping out of the woods behind himself and Kerlew.

"Drop your packs and step aside," a woman in the center directed. She was raw-boned and grizzle-haired, the lines of experience marking her face.

"Of course." Gar slipped out of the straps and let the pack fall. Reluctantly, Kerlew did the same.

"Well, if we've got the goods, we don't need the peddlers anymore," a young man grunted and laid his cheek to his rifle's stock, sighting at Gar.

Gar stepped back and swung his staff up, knocking the outlaw's rifle high. It went off, the bullet clipping twigs from a tree, and the young outlaw shouted in anger.

Behind him, another rifle blasted and a man howled.

"None of that!" a woman cried. "We'll hit each other! Club them!"

A rifle butt came whistling overhand at Gar's head. He pivoted and kicked; the man cried out as he fell.

"None of that!" the woman cried again, and Gar looked up to see an arrow pointed straight at him.

Kerlew gave a cry of defeat and held up both hands.

Gar sidestepped; the archer tracked him. Gar leaped in and the woman loosed. Gar spun aside; the arrow shot past him into another outlaw, who cried out in pain as Gar swung full-armed at the archer's bow. She howled as it jolted against her hand, then fell loose.

Kerlew stared in disbelief. Another outlaw leaped up to hold a dagger to his throat, but Kerlew struck it up as he pulled his own knife.

"Hold!" the woman cried, and the band froze but stayed poised for action.

"Why, Regan?" the young man demanded.

"Don't you see the young one's coat, Jase?" Regan demanded. "It's faded nearly to gray, like ours! That's no clansman, but an outlaw like us!"

The bandits took a closer look, frowning. One or two nodded.

"But the big one, his coat's near new!" the young bandit protested.

"Are you blind?" Regan demanded. "New it may be, but it's no plaid I've ever seen."

"All right, so he's a peddler!" Jase snapped. "That makes him fair game, doesn't it?"

"Not when he has an outcast for a partner." A burly older man shouldered up beside the young one. "How come you be keeping such company, boy?"

Kerlew shrugged. "Two are safer on the road than one, mister, and the peddler, he was good enough to welcome my company."

"There's sense in that." Regan turned to Gar. "We won't steal from you, peddler, but we'll trade—if we've anything you want, that is."

"Fair enough, and a good deal for both," Gar answered. "First, though, what do you say to breaking bread together?"

"You carry bread?" Jase asked, wide-eyed.

"Journeybread," Gar clarified, "but if we soak it awhile, it'll be soft enough to eat. Light a fire, somebody, and I'll brew some tea." He turned to rummage in his pack.

● ● ●

The door opened and three clansfolk came in with a fourth in their midst, a man who wore a jacket of a different tartan and carried a white flag on a three-foot staff. Alea turned to Moira with excitement and hope, but the seer only shook her head, mouth tight against disappointment. Alea turned back, disappointed herself, and saw that the flag was scrupulously made, the cloth stout and the edges serged, but also a bit worn, obviously washed many times. This flag of truce was no harbinger of peace; it was only a device, a convenience in the endless and deadly war of the feuds.

A pathway cleared between the doorway and Grandma, and the sentries marched down it, rifles still at the ready, the stranger holding his chin high and his flag upright. "We've a Cumber come to talk to you, Gram," one of the sentries said.

The Cumber nodded in deference to Grandma's years. "Good day to you, Helen Campbell."

"And to you, Alan Cumber." Grandma's tone could have frozen the duck pond. "To what to we owe the pleasure of this visit?"

No one seemed to notice the irony of the empty social formula. Then Alea glanced at the men and women to each side and realized that it might not have been so empty after all. Whether it was simply a break in the monotony or a genuine pleasure at seeing someone from outside the family, the Campbells really were glad to see Alan Cumber. One of the older women even had a gleam in her eye as she watched him, a gleam dulled by regret. Alea looked at the intruder again, looked beneath the grizzled hair and the lined and weather-beaten skin and saw that Alan Cumber had once been handsome—in fact, that he still was, if you had eyes to see it. A pang of grief shot through Alea, grief for a romance that might have been, grief for the poor woman who had wasted her life in yearning.

"A pleasure it is indeed to see you again," Alan Cumber said gallantly. "I come to ask a favor, though."

"And no little courage it took to come into the stronghold of your enemies." Grandma returned compliment for compliment. "Don't know as how we can do a favor for a Cumber, but some requests we can't refuse out of simple human decency. Is this one of them?"

"It is that, ma'am," Alan said, "for we hear you've a healer come to visit, and our Gram is took sorely ill."

"What, Emily Farland ill?" For a moment, genuine concern and fright showed in Grandma's face before the granite mask stiffened again. "We were girls together, played snap-out at barn dances and sang play-party songs with the others before she turned so addle-brained as to marry a Cumber."

"Yes, you never have had a quarrel with the Farlands, and neither have we," Alan returned equably.

Alea stared, shocked. The neighbors to either side were enemies, but the family one farm away were friends! When she stopped to think about it, it made sense—both Campbells and Cumbers were feuding with the Gregors, and the enemy of their enemy was their friend. But how did they get together to socialize? And how rarely did they see one another, with an enemy in the way? She suddenly realized the lives these people must lead, each clan beleaguered, with an enemy in every direction and no sight of a friend save at special occasions that couldn't come more than a few times a year.

"No, Emily and I had no quarrel, till she married a Cumber," Grandma said, and there were undertones of grief and anger at what she still perceived as a personal betrayal. "Still, I'd do what I can for her in the name of days gone by. Do you wish to ask the healer to come to her, then?"

"That I do."

"There she stands." Grandma gestured toward Alea. "Ask her with our blessing."

Alan Cumber turned to Alea, hat in his hands, and asked gravely, "Ma'am, will you come heal our Grandma?"

Alea stared, confused by the undertones of friendship and caring—no, *need*, need of other people under the mask of the feud.

"Surely you will, won't you Alea?" Moira asked. "You said you'll heal anyone who's ill, after all."

"I said I'll try," Alea corrected her. "There are many sicknesses beyond my knowledge and skill." She turned back to Alan Cumber. "But yes, I'll come. I'll see her and talk to her, and if I can, I'll heal her."

"She don't talk so good any more, ma'am," Alan Cumber said.

Stroke, Alea thought, but beyond Alan Cumber she saw the naked realization of tragedy in Grandma's face.

Then the old lady recovered her composure and turned to look from one side of the great room to another at her children and grandchildren. "Who'll go as escorts to see these ladies safely to Marsh Creek?" She turned back to Alan. "That's where your kinfolk will meet her, isn't it?"

"The boundary between your lands and ours. Yes, ma'am."

Grandma nodded and looked out over the throng. "Who wants to go?"

Half a dozen men and women stepped forward, all of them young. A second behind them, their parents stepped forward, too.

Alea turned to Alan Cumber. "Will you swear by Belenos to bring me back here safely?"

"Or on to the next clan that needs you? Yes, ma'am. I swear it, and that binds all my kin, since I'm their messenger." But Alan Cumber was clearly hiding amusement. Looking about her, Alea saw the same covert smiles on the faces of the Campbells, even Grandma's.

She couldn't ask Moira about it until they were on the road, when the young folks' merriment drew their anxious parents' attention enough so that the two women could speak with a certain measure of privacy. "Moira, why are they amused by taking an oath to Belenos?"

"Why, you know why—because nobody believes in the gods anymore," Moira said with deep regret, "no one save the Druids and a few odd ones like myself, that is."

Alea turned back to the road. "What use is their oath, then?"

"None," Moira said, "but their word is good. In fact, anyone caught breaking his word is liable to exile and outlawry."

Alea stared at her. "Let me see if I understand you. They don't believe in their own gods, but their promises are sacred?"

"Of course," Moria said. "Something has to be."

Gar pulled bread and cheese from his pack and was surprised that the outlaws didn't stare and swallow; they were better fed than the last batch. Now that he noticed, they were better dressed, too; their jackets and trousers were of stout tan home-spun cloth, clean and mended, not the rag-tag worn-out plaids he'd seen before. The hunting must be better in this part of the forest.

One young man gathered some sticks and started a fire with sparks from his flintlock while the other members of the band slowly sat down. The leader took some strips of dried meat from a pocket and offered them to Gar. "It's tasty, if you can chew."

"I haven't lost that many teeth yet." Gar hadn't, in fact, lost any, but he well knew that some of the clansfolk who appeared middle-aged weren't really much older than he—a subsistence society could do that to people. He accepted a stick of jerky and took a bite in proof. It was indeed tasty, had been dried with some sort of spice. These people weren't particularly hungry, but sharing food was a sign of mutual trust. Gar reminded himself that it wasn't an alliance, just a beginning.

"I'm Regan," the woman said. "What have you to trade?"

"Needles, pins, some spices, lace . . . that sort of thing," Gar said.

"Lace?" Regan looked up in surprise. "Where did you get that?"

"Traded for it with an outlaw some miles from here."

"Some miles?" Regan asked, bristling. "How many?"

The bandits muttered darkly.

"Three days' march," Gar said, surprised.

The bandits relaxed, and Regan said, "Too far for us to worry about, then."

"Worry about?" Gar frowned. "They wouldn't be apt to set upon you. After all, you're all outlaws together."

"Not together, stranger," a beefy man said. "A band gets big enough, it's likely to run off the small bands around it—or kill them if they won't run."

Gar stared. "But why?"

"Keep 'em out of the big band's hunting grounds," the man grunted, "keep 'em from poaching." He had the sound of one who knew from experience.

Gar was catching unpleasant echoes of medieval lords' keeping the forests for their own private hunting reserves. "That's wrong. The big bands are treating the small ones as they themselves were, and hated."

"They think that gives them the right," Regan explained, "so the small bands stay well clear of the big ones."

"Water's boiling," the fire-maker reported.

Gar reached in his pack and pulled out a few spoonfuls of powder to sprinkle in the water. The bandits took wooden mugs from under their jackets and handed them over to be filled.

Gar poured and handed them back, then inhaled the steam from his own mug and said, "I would think that shared misery would draw all outlaws together, for company and protection."

Regan shook her head. "Think, peddler. There isn't a one of us who wasn't kicked out of his clan for being untrustworthy. No one wanted to risk their lives depending on a man or woman who might decide it's wrong to fire a gun in battle. How could any of us trust another outlaw, unless she's part of our own band?"

"By respect," Gar said.

Several of the outlaws gave snorts of laughter and Regan smiled. "You think any outlaw from a big band is going to respect some mangy, tattered loner who isn't even a good enough shot to be welcomed by a large band?"

"Of course," Gar said, "because she's human."

Now Regan snorted, too. "You don't respect someone just for that, peddler."

"You should," Gar said, "because it's a rare person indeed who doesn't have some sort of talent—and the ones who are really that incompetent are too feeble to dare to talk back to their clansfolk, or to risk going to the woods alone. Just being an outlaw at all, in a clan world like this, means you have to have some talents worth respecting."

"Or that you're such a weakling that your own kin didn't want to be lumbered with you!" Jase said hotly.

"How many of you have ever heard of someone being cast out for that?" Gar asked.

The outlaws frowned, exchanged glances, muttered to one another, but no one answered.

Gar nodded. "I thought not. Even a half-wit is put to work cleaning the barns—and doesn't believe in himself enough to believe in his own ideas, if he comes up with any. If you keep an open mind about everyone you meet, if you're careful not to condemn them without knowing anything about them, you'll find you can respect them—and that respect is enough for the start of an alliance, at least. Then you take on small tasks together to find out how far you can trust one another—and if you find you can, you tackle bigger and bigger jobs together until you do trust one another."

The outlaws exchanged frowns, uncertain, but Regan gave Gar a sardonic smile. "Sounds pretty, but you don't for a moment think it could work, do you?"

"Aye," said Jase, and turned to Kerlew. "What talent have you, single man?"

Kerlew flushed at the tone of insult, but before he could answer, Gar said, "Look at it this way, then. Think of a boy you knew when you were a lad, the one who could never catch a ball or shoot straight, the one who was always last to be chosen for a game."

Most of the outlaws grunted, smiles tight with assurance of their own superiority.

"Sometimes those boys grow up to become . . ." Gar tried to think what this culture would call a wizard—"conjure men. Would you want him to have a score to settle with you if he did?"

The outlaws lost their smiles at that, but Regan gave him a skeptical and scornful look. "Conjure men? You don't really believe in such, do you?"

But she spoke too easily, with too much mockery—all bravado. She was whistling in the dark, trying to assure herself that such things didn't exist, and Gar could hear the undertone in her voice, the echo in her thoughts, the fear of the unknown. "You never know," he said. "You never know."

"Enough of such stuff." Regan dashed the dregs of her tea into the fire, then stood and began kicking dirt onto the flames. "The day's far enough gone already, and us with no game to show for it. Let's head back to camp and find what meat we can on the way." She looked down at Gar. "You can come along, peddler—both of you. We were too quick to jump you, so let us make it up a little, at least, with dinner and a bed for the night."

Alarm stiffened Kerlew's back. "I don't know—it's not on our way . . ."

"But if they've furs or amber to trade, it's worth the trip." Gar stood too, shouldering his pack. "I'll be glad of your hospitality, Regan." He turned back to Kerlew. "You don't have to come along, Kerlew. You're your own man, you know."

"Oh, I know that right enough." Kerlew stood, too. "But I've few enough friends left in the world, and I'm not about to desert a new one. Let's go."

The keeping room in the Cumbers' great house was darkened and gloomy, only the fire and a few candles lit. The clansfolk sat around the walls on handmade straight chairs and the few pieces of padded furniture, anxious or, in some cases, already resigned to Grandma's passing. The younger children were in bed, but a few of the older ones sat up with their parents, nodding with weariness but fighting sleep.

A woman whose auburn hair was streaked with silver came

up to them, proffering a hand. "I'm Achalla Cumber. Will you come to my mother now?"

"Gladly," said Alea. "Lead us, please."

Achalla turned away, and Alea followed, slipping through the gloom with Moira, stepping as softly as they might, following the older woman through a doorway to the side of the fireplace. They came into a room lit only by a candle on a bedstand, illuminating the pale, wrinkled face of Emily Cumber. Her cheeks seemed sunken, her whole face drawn, the eyes staring fever-bright, looking at the ceiling.

The clanswoman stepped up to her bedside, saying softly, "There's a healer come to see you, Gram."

The old woman's eyes swiveled to Alea—or one of them did. The other tried, but barely moved. Alea sat down on the bed, taking the old woman's hand. Shriveled and wrinkled, it felt more like a claw. Emily Cumber tried to speak to her, but all that came out was a sort of cawing.

Alea's heart sank; she knew the signs of stroke when she saw them. Grandma wouldn't die of this one episode, of course, but Alea felt certain there were other blood clots waiting to break free into her bloodstream and hit her brain. For a moment, Alea yearned for the new and wonderful medicines she'd read of in Herkimer's databanks—blood thinners, sonic beams to destroy the clots, nerve regeneration serum—but knew she'd never have them.

Grandma gabbled at her again. Alea couldn't understand the words, but she read the old woman's thoughts: *Don't waste your time, child. My days are numbered, and there's only hours left.*

Alea passed her hands over the woman's body and felt signs of sickness and decay there. Was it her imagination, or was this really a psi power she hadn't known she had?

13

Alea's mind raced, seeking words of comfort, racking through what she'd read of Celtic mythology. "You've lived a good life, haven't you, ma'am?"

Emily froze, staring at her; then her eyes lost focus, and Alea knew she was looking back into the past, to the parties and socials of her youth, to her beloved Whitman courting her, the births of her children, the years of long work and little rest caring for them, the fear of battle, the agony when she was wounded, the panic when Whitman took a bullet and lay so long near death, the joy at his recovery, the marriages of their children, the births of their grandchildren, then the agony and grief of Whitman's death, leaving her heart frozen. Not long after, she'd felt completely swamped by her own Mother Cumber's dying and passing the care of her brood on to Emily, who stood fast though she knew she couldn't be strong enough, couldn't be wise enough, but hang it, she had managed, had led wisely, and her children and grandchildren still lived, still prospered, and their love and care had finally thawed the frost around her heart . . .

Her eyes focused again on Alea's; she gave a little nod. *Yes. It was good.*

"Well, then, you've nothing to fear from death." Alea pressed her hand. "If your soul's born again, it will be to an even better life than this—and if you cross the river and come to the Afterworld, you'll find it a place of peace and love and plenty."

Emily Cumber stared at her in disbelief. *Could they be true? Could all those children's tales be true?*

"They're tales for us all, not for children alone." Alea patted her hand. "Remember Danu; remember Toutatis; remember the one god whom we see in a thousand forms. There's peace there, and comfort—and Whitman waiting."

Hope kindled in the old woman's eyes.

By the door, her daughter watched in amazement.

Alea talked long then, telling her again the tales of her childhood, the myths of gods and goddesses in which she had ceased to believe. Now, though, at the brink of death, the gateway to the undiscovered country, she listened with almost desperate attention, eager for the words of hope that she had forgotten for so many years.

When Alea's voice grew hoarse, Moira took up where she left off, until finally the old woman gestured her to silence, then beckoned to her daughter and cawed something incomprehensible. Achalla looked to Alea and the healer told her, "She bids you summon all the clan to her bedside now."

Achalla stared at her mother a moment, then turned and hurried out of the room.

Alea and Moira sat by the old woman, one holding each hand, until her children and grandchildren began to file into the room. As it grew crowded, Alea relinquished Emily's hand and stepped back into the shadows, Moira with her.

Emily Cumber didn't speak, only raised her hands in blessing, eyes locking one by one with each of her brood. Then, finally, she beckoned weakly to her eldest daughter. Slowly,

Achalla came to her bedside and knelt. Emily laid her hand on Achalla's head and cawed to her brood in a tone of command.

Alea spoke up from the shadows. "She says that Achalla shall be your grandmother now, all of you, and care for you in Emily Cumber's place."

Fear shone in Achalla's eyes, fear of the awesome responsibility, and she clutched at Emily's hand. "Don't leave us, Gram! We're lost without you! *I'm* lost!"

But Emily only shook her head an inch to each side, smiling with affection, fairly radiating love—and, so loving, her eyes dulled, and she died.

Regan led them out of the woods and gestured at a clearing. "Here's home."

Gar and Kerlew stared. The clearing had been widened by axe and saw, more than a hundred yards across; stumps stood all about it. The logs had been stacked to form cabins, chinked with mud and thatched with brush. They stood in a circle around a broad swath of lawn where goats and sheep grazed.

"This is no camp—this a village!" Kerlew blurted.

"A village it is, a hundred fifty men and women, some of them born and grown here, and thirty children—so all that stops us from being a clan is kinship." Regan turned, her rifle leveled at Gar's midriff. "But we're marrying one another, and the children will be kin soon enough. We're calling ourselves the Weald clan—it's an old name for a big forest—and we don't have much use for small bands."

"Even less for loners." Jase gave Kerlew a slap that skimmed the top of his head. Kerlew's head snapped back; he turned to glare at the youth.

"Oh, you'd wish our Jase ill, would you?" said a young woman, and gave Kerlew another slap.

"What are you staring at, big man?" Regan reached up to backhand Gar across the cheek. "You'll give us your wares now, and no trading about it!"

"Yeah!" said an older man. "You want respect? Here's the

respect a loner gets." He slammed a kick at Gar's shin.

Gar sidestepped, but the glancing blow connected enough to hurt. "What are you talking about? The clans honor peddlers! Nobody will hurt them because they need the goods we trade!"

"We're an outlaw clan," another middle-aged woman said, striding up to him. "We make our own rules." She slammed a punch at Gar's belly.

Gar blocked it without thinking. "What about hospitality? We're your guests!"

"Guests, aye, but we didn't say you wouldn't have to pay for your food and lodging," Regan sneered.

"Just hand us your pack—that will do for your fee," a younger woman said, then turned on Kerlew. "Him, though, we'll use for sport."

"Which part of him do you want, cousin?" another young woman asked with a grin.

"Off with you!" Kerlew stepped back, but waved them away, too, glaring. "Or I'll lay a satire on you!"

The whole band burst out laughing.

"Oh yes, let's hear your satire, my lad," an older woman wheezed, wiping her eyes. "It must be a good one; you've got us laughing before you begin!"

"Oh, I'm so afraid," Jase sneered, and the others chorused agreement.

"Afraid you should be," Kerlew said, his face grim, and began to chant,

> *"The girls of Weald, they must be*
> *The ugliest ones in the whole country.*
> *Hooks out for lads who near them stray*
> *For none would gladly with them stay!"*

The girls shouted with anger and pressed in.

Alarmed, Gar started reaching out with his mind for sticks and rifle stocks.

"Arla! Your face is changing!" one of the girls cried.

Arla looked at her and screamed. "Am I like you, Betsy? Oh, I hope not!"

"Why?" Betsy asked in panic. "What do I look like?"

"Your nose is growing into a hook and your jaw into a nut-cracker!" Arla cried. "You've warts all over!"

Gar stared but could only see the pleasant features each girl had naturally. They, though, were obviously seeing something else.

"Give us back our faces, sorcerer!" a third girl screamed and lifted her rifle.

"Beware!" Gar cried. "He can't lift the spell if he's dead!"

"Curse you!" the girl cried, dropping her rifle, and went for Kerlew with her bare hands.

Kerlew was stunned but had enough presence of mind to duck and dodge, finding breath to cry,

> "Beauty is as beauty does,
> Ladies loving as turtledoves,
> But girls of spite and malice show
> Witch's features, twisted so!
>
> "Let folk who can't let others live,
> Suffer aches that they would give!
> Kicks and slaps they'll aim in vain,
> And feel what they would give in pain!"

Heads rocked all throughout the band; people cried out, hurt and angry. Several hopped on one foot.

"He's doing it!" Regan cried in disbelief. "He's causing us the pain he speaks of!"

The whole band drew back in awe and fear.

"Now, Kerlew! The woods!" Gar snapped.

The two men whirled and dashed into the trees.

Behind them, the band came alive with one massed shout and crashed into the underbrush behind them.

• • •

Alea wept, quietly but openly and without shame, as the room slowly emptied. When only Achalla was left with a younger woman by her side—her own daughter, Alea guessed—she let Moira lead her from the room.

"There now, you did all you could," the seer assured her in a soothing tone. "More than most would have been able to do, I'm sure."

"But not enough!"

"More than enough," Moira said, "and I'm sure all her kin will think so, too."

"Her kin!" Alea looked up, their predicament suddenly breaking in on her grief. Eyes still reddened and teary, she said, "They'll be outraged with me now. I was supposed to heal her, and there she lies dead!"

"Now, they'll do no such thing," Moira said with an edge of sternness to her voice. "You told them you might not be able to heal her, after all."

"That's so, but they expected it nonetheless." Alea saw Achalla coming out of her grandmother's bedroom and rose, bracing herself for the worst. She had some ability at telekinesis, after all—she could make hot coals fly from the fireplace, let the rifles' hammers fall, distract them in a dozen ways while she and Moira fled to the door, where her staff stood against the jamb, then out.

First, though, she had to confront Achalla. She blotted her eyes on her sleeve, then squared her shoulders and stood, braced, as the room quieted about them and Achalla advanced on her slowly.

Five feet from her, the new Grandmother of the Cumber clan stopped and inclined her head. "Great thanks we must give you, Lady Healer, and you, Lady Seer, for the consolation you have given our Grandmother in her last hour."

Alea stood staring, dumbfounded.

"We are glad to have done what little we can," Moira answered.

"Yes . . . yes, of course," Alea said, then burst out, "but it was so little!"

"Not little at all." Achalla answered with a melancholy smile. "She was in terror of death till you came. You gave her courage and a sweet passage, lady. And of no smaller moment, you gave her the tranquility to appoint her successor." The new Grandmother shuddered. "Though I don't know if I'm equal to the task."

"Neither was she, when it came upon her," Alea said without thinking.

Achalla frowned, wondering how Alea could know that, but she was distracted by voices on every side crying,

"Indeed you can, Achalla!"

"Of course you can, my dear!"

"Hail Grandmother Achalla Cumber!"

"Well, I've only the one grandchild yet," Achalla answered with a tremulous smile, "but your confidence warms me."

"We're all your grandchildren now!" a young man said stoutly.

"So speaks my son-in-law," Achalla said with quiet pride, then turned back to Alea again. "See how well you have wrought, lady! This clan shall continue and prosper now, for in her death, Grandmother has made us all one, thanks to the strength you gave her."

"Not me, but the goddesses." The words seemed to come automatically, even from outside Alea.

"Even as you say." Achalla bent her head again. "I could almost believe in them again, after seeing the magic they wrought in Gram."

"Believe in them indeed," Moira said, her voice low but carrying, "when dark hours come and your world seems to break apart around you, for then the gods and goddesses of our ancestors will make it whole again."

Achalla turned to her with a slight frown and a longing to believe, but all she said was, "So may it be."

She turned back to Alea. "Ask of us what you will, lady, and if it is within our power, you shall have it."

Alea managed a weak smile. "A night's lodging, and breakfast in the morning, then the escort Alan Cumber pledged in all your names, for you have given me the hope that I may still heal the sick."

"I shall go with her!" a young man cried.

"And I!" a young woman said eagerly.

"And I!"

"And I!"

"And I!"

"I claim the right to lead this escort," Alan said gravely, "for it was I who promised it."

"And so you shall," Achalla told him. "Now, though, pour mead and break soul-cakes together, and say each what you remember most fondly of Grandmother Emily Cumber!"

Then the wake began and lasted far into the night. At least, Alea thought it did, she went to bed exhausted before more than an hour or two had passed.

Gar and Kerlew crashed through the underbrush, then broke through onto a carpet of brown needles beneath towering evergreens.

"Zigzag!" Gar called. "Run straight and you're easier to hit!"

"Known that since I was five!" Kerlew snapped, and ran.

They twisted back and forth between the trunks, horribly exposed. Any sharpshooter could have sighted them and had a clear field of fire, if he could have known which way they would zag next—and if he'd been near. But Gar reached out with his mind, twisting senses of orientation, and behind them voices called out to one another, shouting contradictory directions.

"North! I hear them crashing about!"

"East! See where the brush is broken!"

"Footsteps! I see them clearly! Run west!"

"South! I hear them calling to each other!"

"Calling?" Kerlew gasped. "We've been . . . silent!"

"Not now . . . you're . . . not!" Gar panted. "Run!"

They ran, in and out among the trunks. Finally the evergreens gave out and they blundered in among oaks and elms. Still they ran, hopping over low growth and crashing through bushes until a stream cut across their path.

"Rest!" Kerlew fell to his knees, gasping. "Streams are . . . boundaries!"

They collapsed, gasping, listening for sounds of pursuit but hearing none—though Gar, opening his mind for thoughts, could hear loud arguments about which way the peddlers had gone. He threw in a few more false clues to keep them arguing.

"How could they . . . fail to find us?" Kerlew wheezed. "These are . . . their woods!"

"They didn't expect us to run," Gar said airily. He caught another breath and said, "They probably spent . . . long enough screaming in shock . . . at your satire . . . that they couldn't tell . . . where we'd gone."

Kerlew frowned. "I've never seen satires really hurt people before. Not right away, anyway."

"Not right away?" Gar gave him a keen glance. "When did they work?"

"Within a week—at least, it would start that quickly. Just bad luck, tripping over things, missing a shot, that sort of trouble."

Gar nodded. "The satire convinced them they'd have bad luck, so their minds made them have accidents. How often have you laid a satire before, Kerlew?"

"Only the once," Kerlew said, "against Grandpa, when he cast me out of my clan, but I couldn't stay to see what happened, of course. I didn't think anything had."

"Oh, really?" Gar asked with foreboding. "What punishment did you lay?"

"One that fit the crime. He'd a mind to cast me out for speaking for peace, so I said he'd never know peace of mind again."

Gar thought of the old man constantly worried, constantly

fearing something bad would happen, constantly tormented by memories of his past cruelties and fearing revenge, and shuddered. There was no question in his own mind—Kerlew was a powerful esper who didn't know his own nature. He was a projective telepath who could make people think they saw things that weren't real, could send their minds into turmoil, and probably make their subconscious minds cause them to trip over their own feet or—worse for these people—jerk the rifle a little whenever they pulled the trigger so they'd begin to miss every shot. He turned to Kerlew. "We're away and safe. Maybe you could give the girls back their beauty."

"Well, I suppose there's no harm in it," Kerlew said doubtfully. He thought a moment, then chanted,

> *"They who watch but never care,*
> *Let them see what's really there,*
> *Though, mindful of the pain they've felt,*
> *Grow kind where wounding hurt they've dealt."*

"They'll see themselves as they really are now?" Gar asked.

Kerlew nodded. "If my words have any real power, they will."

"You didn't tell me you could make verses that would shame and hurt people."

"The shame I knew about," Kerlew muttered. "The hurt, I didn't." He shivered. "I never dreamed a satire could really do anything but embarrass!"

"Perhaps you never spoke it with such emotion before," Gar suggested. "You might want to think about forgiving your grandfather."

"Him? Never!" Kerlew's face hardened. "The pain he's cost by his ridiculing and raging, the dear ones he's cast out—if my words hurt him at all, it was too little."

Gar decided it was too early to tell the boy that his grudge really hurt himself more than his grandfather, that it kept him tied to the events that had caused him so much pain and waked the fear and humiliation again and again whenever he thought of them. If Kerlew could ever summon the courage to face the damage that trauma had done, grieve for it, then accept himself in spite of it, there would come a time when he would be able to forgive and cut himself free of the pain—but not yet, it seemed, not yet.

Suddenly a distant yelping broke out. Kerlew leaped to his feet. "The hounds! They haven't given up! Cross that river, quickly!"

"Find a ford!" Gar snapped.

They turned upstream and jogged along, watching the depth of the water. The brush thickened. Gar was about to cast aside his pack and swim when they suddenly broke through some bushes and found themselves in serenity.

It was a ring of lawn sixty yards across with a huge mound in its center. Goats and sheep grazed the clearing and the slopes, demonstrating how the grass was kept so neatly trimmed. At the eastern edge stood a small cottage, stucco plastered over wattle and daub, beams showing in half-timbering, thatched with straw, and bordered by flowering bushes.

Kerlew froze and stared. "A Mound! We can't stay here!"

"Why not?" Gar asked.

"Because fairies live inside it and there's no telling what new mischief they'll dream up for the man who intrudes on them! Quickly, Gar! Turn and go!"

He spun about, but the breeze shifted and blew the belling of the hounds more loudly to him. Kerlew froze.

14

Gar reached out a restraining hand. "Wait a minute. You know that dream of fairies and elves I had?"

"The Old Ones? Aye." Kerlew turned to him, puzzled. "What of them?"

"They told me that if ever I were in trouble, I could go to the Keepers of the Mounds for sanctuary. Do you think we're in trouble?"

Kerlew glanced over his shoulder at the distant clamor. "I think you could say that, yes."

"Then let's throw ourselves on the mercy of the Keepers." Gar started toward the cottage.

Kerlew stared after him as though he were crazy. Then he shrugged and followed.

Before Gar could knock, the door opened to reveal an old woman and old man, wrinkled faces creased with smiles, white hair straight and flowing (though most of the old man's was in his beard) and a deep serenity in their eyes. "Welcome, travelers," said the woman. "How come you to the Hollow Hill?"

"By great good fortune," Gar told her, "and hard beset by a band of outlaws."

The old man raised his head. "Yes, I hear their hounds."

Gar frowned. "Don't you fear them?"

The old man turned his head from side to side, still smiling. "None dare to come here with ill will, for the fairies would lame them in an instant or the elves lay them low with elf-shot."

"If you need protection from them, you shall have it," the old woman said, "if you do not fear the fairies."

"Which you would be well advised to do," the old man warned.

"*You* do not," Kerlew pointed out.

"True." The old couple exchanged a warm glance; then the woman turned to Kerlew and explained, "We fled our clans so that we might wed, but they tracked us down, even as they track you right now, and in our flight, we blundered upon this mound in the dead of night. We lay there gasping in each other's arms, not fearing, for we thought that whatever harm the fairies might render could certainly be no worse than what our kin might do."

"And the fairies spared you?" Kerlew asked, wide-eyed.

The old man nodded. "We did not even have to ask. They came out and knew us at sight for desperate lovers whose romance defied the hatred of our clans. When our kindred burst from the woods, they found us surrounded by a glowing cloud of fairies, who bade them touch us at their peril."

"They halted then, and conferred," the old woman said, "and told the fairies that we would be safe, so long as we never left this clearing. Thereupon the Old Ones declared us the Keepers of the Mound, and we dwelt with the old Keeper and cared for him in his age until he died, then lived here most happily . . ."

"Well, Joram, there have been arguments," his wife reminded him.

"There have indeed, Maeve, and times when we chafed at our bondage and wished we could visit our kinfolk," Joram admitted, "but it would have been death for me if her clan had found me, and shame for her."

"No, we have been happy here far more often than not," Maeve told Gar and Kerlew. "Seven babes have I borne . . ." Sadness touched her face. ". . . and three buried." Then she brightened again. "But four did we rear to manhood and womanhood, and ever and anon they come back to stay awhile with us."

"Where could they have gone?" Gar asked in surprise.

"To any clan who didn't know theirs," Kerlew told him, "ones many miles away."

"Even so." Maeve nodded. "My Brilla, she married Josh Farland, and Orlin, he wed Beryl Gonigle. Finn went to study with a Druid and came back a bard. He still studies, and will be a Druid himself one day."

"Moira, though, has a heavy weird," Joram said, frowning.

"Aye, my Moira was touched by the goddesses," Maeve sighed. "Myself, I scarcely believed in them, but she went past belief—she knew they were real. She had a vision of a man and woman who came to bring peace to all the clans—only the first vision of many—and has gone to tramp the roadways looking for them, preaching peace and forgiveness to all the clans, even to the outlaws."

"I fear for her safety," Joram said with a heavy frown, "but I cannot go to guard her—I am bound here by the hatred of our clans."

"I had never known," Kerlew said softly, almost in a whisper. "I had heard of the Keepers of the Mounds, but I never dreamt that they themselves sought sanctuary in these clearings."

"If the rest are like to us, they are happy enough at it," Maeve said with a smile. "So we herd our goats and tend our sheep, and see to it that the shrubs are pruned and the grass kept short for the fairy folk to dance upon, and wait for our Moira to find her true love and come back to take up our vigil."

"Brigid grant she does!" Joram said fervently.

"For your sakes, I hope so," Gar said, "hope so indeed. But surely the Wee Folk don't really need human caretakers for their hills!"

"I suppose not," Joram said, "but they do need someone to

speak for them to the clansfolk now and again, and we New Folk have need of someone to keep good relations with the Old Ones, whether our kin know it or not."

"I have heard they can drive a mortal mad," Kerlew said, his voice low and shaking.

"They can indeed," Maeve assured him, "though it takes a whole band of fairies to wrench at the mind of one single person. Naetheless, given time enough, they could drive us all mad, and therefore do our clans honor our sanctuary, so that someone may be near to convince fairies and elves alike that not all New Folk are villains."

"A hard task that is, when we are so busy slaying one another," Kerlew said darkly.

"Surely not all the Keepers are outcast lovers," Gar said tentatively.

"They are not," Maeve confirmed. "The Wee Folk tell us that most are couples in their middle years, who have lost several of their children—some even all—to the constant battles that are ever brewing. When they can no longer endure it, they speak out against the feuds and are therefore cast out of their clans."

"It sounds as though many clansfolk hate the fighting," Gar said.

"Very many indeed." Maeve nodded. "But few have the courage to speak up."

Gar and Kerlew slept that night in the moon shadow of the mound, and perhaps it was the fairy folk who put the dreams into Gar's head, or perhaps it was simply the talk with the Keepers, but Gar dreamt indeed, dreamt all night through, of aged and wrinkled faces, of younger faces slashed with the scars of war, of people of all ages whose bodies bore horrid wounds— and they spoke.

First came an old man, gaunt and grim, who swam out of the darkness behind Gar's eyes and glared down at him, demanding, "Why do you sleep here when there is work for you to do?"

"Because I'll work much better if I'm rested," Gar answered reasonably, "but what work is this you speak of?"

"Peace!" the old man thundered. "My great-great-great-grand-children are still dying because of my great-great-great-great-great-grandfather's stupid mistake and more stupid pride! You have the ideas and the knowledge to stop the feuds—why do you lie here idle?"

"These things take time," Gar temporized. "Besides, I don't have the ideas and I'm not sure I have the knowledge."

"You have both!" It was a young woman, a ragged, dark-rimmed hole in her jacket over the heart, eyes blazing. "You know enough about us all and our clans, you know enough about the Wee Folk, and your own guardian will aid them! I never had children because this idiotic feud killed me too soon! Stop it and give a chance of life to what are left of my kin!"

She turned away, revealing the huge, horrible exit wound, and another face swam up in her place—an old man with a nutcracker chin and grim, accusing eye. "You've heard of the Druids, the Old Ones have pledged to aid you, and your own guardian spirit will work with them to aid your cause!"

"What guardian spirit?" Gar asked, frowning.

The ghost went on as though he hadn't heard. "You know the feuds started because there was no law! You know the clans all honor some laws!"

"Yes, but not the ones that punish murderers," Gar pointed out.

A fourth face swam near, a woman in middle years with a mole in the center of her forehead. Looking again, Gar could see it was a bullet hole. "You only need to find some sort of law they will all embrace!" she cried.

"What law could that be?"

She, too, didn't seem to hear his question. "Make your law, then, and send the outlaws to bear word of it to all the clans!"

"The outlaws? They'll be shot on sight! And who will enforce this law?"

"The Old Ones, as they have pledged to aid you—and it is they who shall protect your outlaw couriers!"

She started to turn away; Gar shuddered at the thought of seeing the exit wound, but a young man's face swam up in place of hers, his eyes burning, a raw gash furrowing his cheek—fortunately, his chest wasn't visible. "I never lived to see my baby born! From beyond the grave I watched him grow and saw him cut down in battle before he was twenty! How many more fatherless sons must there be before you will act?"

"But I don't know enough yet—"

"See what will happen if you don't!" The young man's face swept aside, revealing a meadow surrounded by evergreens, morning mist rising from the long grass. Three clansfolk stepped out into it, warily, looking about them, rifles poised.

A volley of gunfire erupted from the trees ahead of them. They screamed and fell, blood thinning with the dew. Rifle fire blasted from the forest behind them; one or two people screamed from the far side of the meadow and rose into view, spinning about, hands clasped to their chests, and fell.

"Murderers!" cried a voice from the far side. "You've slain our children!"

"Assassins! You've slain our young!" someone called nearby. "Retreat or be blasted!"

But the enemy had reloaded and another volley shattered the peace of the forest. The near clan answered it, and in minutes the meadow was filled with gun smoke. Clansfolk came charging through it, dimly seen, only to be slammed back by rifle fire from the near side. But the bullets were spent now, and clansfolk came charging out to batter at each other with rifle stocks. Here and there, reloaded rifles roared, one or two pistols lit the smoke with lurid flashes, men and women screamed, and dimly seen bodies fell as the smoke thickened, hiding all from Gar's sight, muffling the gunshots and the screams, making them dwindle away.

"That's what will happen if you do not act!" a chorus of ghostly voices called. "That's what will happen again and again and again, thousands upon thousands of times!"

With a shudder, Gar sat up.

He looked about him at the gray light of false dawn and realized he'd slept the night through, if you could call that sleep. On the other side of the campfire, Kerlew was sitting up, staring at Gar warily. "You cried out in your sleep."

"Did I really?" Gar pushed himself to his feet. "Only a bad dream." At least, he hoped it was only a dream. He shoved sticks into the coals and blew on them until flames licked up along the bark. "Let's have a hot drink and a little food and be on our way."

They ate, then thanked their hosts the Keepers and set out along a game trail.

"What did you dream?" Kerlew asked.

"You don't want to know," Gar said.

"Perhaps not, but I think I must." Kerlew paled perceptibly, but his chin firmed.

Gar gave him a speculative glance, then said, "As you wish. I dreamed of the ghosts of people who died in this feuding."

Kerlew paled further. "Of which clans?"

"Many," Gar said, "and every single one of them told me to stop dawdling and start making peace, so that their descendants wouldn't have to undergo the misery they had suffered."

"A strong argument."

"Not so strong as the wounds each bore, and the scene of battle they showed me, one of the many battles that would happen if I couldn't stop the fighting." He turned to frown at Kerlew. "How do you suppose they could guess what such a battle would be like?"

Kerlew shrugged. "Memory, I suppose. I don't reckon things have changed much since our ancestors started shooting at one another."

"Yes," Gar said slowly. "A future battle would look much like a past one, wouldn't it?" Unless someone invented a machine gun. He shuddered at the thought.

"Gunfire is gunfire," Kerlew said. "But how do these ghosts expect you to stop the fighting?"

"Invent a law banning feuds, and have the outlaws carry word of it to all the clans."

"They'd be shot dead in their tracks!"

"Not if the Old Ones protected them. At least, that's what the ghosts said."

Kerlew turned thoughtful, then nodded judiciously. "That's so. All it would need would be one elf-shot at a man taking aim at a courier and he'd be left alone. Word would run through the clans like wildfire." He turned back to Gar. "Your couriers would have to carry a white flag, of course."

Gar stared at him. "You're taking this seriously!"

"Why not? It's what I've wanted my whole life—what I was cast out for speaking of. But who would punish a whole clan that broke your law?"

"Again, the Wee Folk—or so said your ancestors."

"The clans might heed the Old Ones at that," Kerlew said thoughtfully. "Surely they wouldn't all drop dead at a fairy's word, but if one after another died or went spastic, they'd mark what the Old Ones said." He turned back to Gar, hope alight in his eyes. "What law would you make?"

"That," Gar said, "is the flaw in the scheme. I haven't the faintest idea."

Kerlew stared at him, the flame of hope guttering, but before it could turn to ashes, the game trail broke out into an actual road, and they saw a dozen clansfolk coming toward them.

"Outlaw!" the strangers cried, and rifles leveled at them, but one of the women cried, "Gar!" and ran to meet him.

Staring, Gar saw Alea, and just had time to wonder if the Old Ones had been directing his steps before she threw her arms about him and pressed her head into his shoulder. "Thank Heavens we've met!"

"I don't think it was Heaven who brought it about." Gar

smiled down at her. "But whoever it was, I'm very grateful to them."

Alea stepped away from him, beaming up into his face. "I've so much to tell you!"

"Lady, is he to be trusted?" asked one of the older clansfolk.

"With my life." She spun to face them. "He's a healer, too."

Kerlew looked up at him in surprise.

"More than that." Moira stepped forward, a weird, distant look on her face. "This is the other I've foreseen, the second of the two who will knit up the wounds of war and bring peace to this poor, sad world."

"Is he indeed!" cried Rowena.

"A peace-preacher? We can't have that!" cried another.

"Outlaw!" cried a third. "His clan has cast him out for weakening their wills to fight!"

But they spoke with too much force or too little, eyeing one another out of the corners of their eyes to make sure their protests were noticed. It didn't take telepathy for Gar and Alea to realize that hope soared in most of their breasts when they heard Moira's prophecy. Only a few of the younger ones spoke with the fire of zeal, and one of the older ones with the flaring of hatred.

"This is my companion, Kerlew," Gar said, gesturing to the young man.

"A pleasure to meet you, Kerlew." Alea turned back to beckon. "And this is my companion, Moira."

A young, dark-haired woman came forward with a tentative smile, eyeing the two men warily.

Kerlew stared at her, and Gar was suddenly sure nothing else seemed to exist for the young man.

Moira frowned at him as though wondering if he'd lost his wits. Then her eyes widened and she stared even as he did.

Alea smiled, amused. "I think they'll get along." She turned back to her escort. "Thank you so much for your protection, Rowena, but I'll be safe enough now."

"With only two men to guard you?" Rowena cried, scandalized. "And one of them an outlaw?"

"And the other not even carrying a rifle," one of the younger men said, lip curling.

"He can do more without a rifle than most men can with one." Alea smiled. "Don't worry, I'll be perfectly safe."

"A man who can outfight a rifle barehanded?" The young man grinned. "This I'd like to see!"

"No you don't," Rowena barked. "Back into place, now!" She turned to Alea, uncertain. "Are you sure, Lady Healer?"

"I am, Rowena." Alea rested a hand on Gar's arm, smiling. "Thank you for bringing us here, but there's no reason to take you away from your homestead any longer. May you have a good journey home."

"If you say so," Rowena said dubiously, then glared at Gar. "If any harm comes to her, lad, you'll have three clans to answer to!"

"She'll be as safe as though she were in a fortress," Gar assured Rowena solemnly.

"All right, then, we'll leave you with her." Rowena turned to press Alea's hand. "Long life to you, lady!"

"And to you, Lady Warrior." Alea smiled. "And tell Achalla I wish her long life, and your clan prosperity."

"I shall." Rowena couldn't help a smile. "Farewell, then."

They watched the clan out of sight. Then Alea spun to Gar. "Now! Tell me everything you've seen, face to face, for there's so much you leave out of your thoughts!" Then she remembered their company and glanced to see if either Kerlew or Moira had heard—but they were still staring at one another, just beginning to move again. Alea smiled and drew Gar far enough away so that the others wouldn't hear unless they stopped talking, which she didn't expect. "Now!" She folded her legs, sitting down on the grass and tucking her skirts under her. "You're looking like a man with a weird. What has happened to make you so?"

"Only dreams," Gar said slowly, and began to tell her about

the Old Ones, then about the Keepers and, finally, about his dream.

When he finished, Alea nodded soberly, thinking.

"It does make sense," Gar admitted. "Since the feuds started when the law broke down, re-establishing law is the only chance of ending the feuds. The problem, of course, is to invent a law that the clans would all accept, when there is no law that binds them all."

"Oh, there is," Alea said slowly, "but they no longer respect it."

"They will if it's enforced by elves and fairies," Gar said, frowning. "What sort of law is this?"

15

Religious law," Alea said.

Gar stared. "You mean they have a religion? I haven't seen many signs of it."

"You've been going among the bandits," Alea said. "I've been going from homestead to homestead as a healer, so I met a priest who had also come to heal. He taught me a few techniques and quite a bit about the local herbs, too."

"Did he really! And what sort of priest is he?"

"A Druid," Alea said, "though I suspect the religion he practices has grown in ways that the Druids of Caesar's time wouldn't recognize."

"Still, religion is religion," Gar said, frowning in thought, "and if it's devoted to goodness and growth, it's a tremendous binding force for a people."

"Devoted to goodness and growth? It is."

"But if they had that much law to hold them together, how did the feuds start?"

"Because they stopped believing in their gods," Alea said, "and began to think of their myths as only charming fairy stories for their children."

"Fairy stories . . ." Gar gazed off into space. "But fairies are real here, and elves, too. I haven't met anyone who doesn't believe in them—including me."

"And me," Alea said with a smile, then realized the thrust of his thought. "You're saying the Druids should include the Old Ones in their religion! Then the clans would have to believe in it!"

"And its laws." Gar nodded. "It shouldn't be hard, after all. The elves and fairies of Ireland were disguised memories of the Celtic gods."

"But how are we to do that?" Alea frowned. "We can't go to all the Druids in the land and ask them to modify their religion to suit us!"

"No, we can't." Gar bit his lip in frustration. "Do you suppose the Wee Folk could also act as a communications net for us, spreading the idea?"

"They probably would, but there's no need," Alea said. "I've found that news travels between these clans with amazing speed. No enmity in the world will keep them from listening to juicy gossip."

Gar stared. "So if one Druid can lay down the law to one clan and see it enforced, all the clans will hear of it?"

"And their Druids with them. Yes." Alea nodded. "But how long will it take you to argue one Druid into accepting elves in his pantheon?"

"As long as it takes me to make a Druid suit." Gar grinned.

Alea stared. "You're not going to impersonate a priest!"

"Why not?" Gar asked. "I've posed as a madman, a peddler, a soldier, and Heaven knows what else as I've gone from planet to planet. Why not a cleric?"

"There's a little matter of knowledge!"

"Yes." Gar nodded. "There, you'll have to teach me what the locals believe."

"But I only know a little. Although . . ." Alea's gaze strayed to Moira.

"You think you might know where you can find out?" Gar prompted.

Moira, though, didn't notice their gazes; she was far too thoroughly caught up in her own conversation.

She and Kerlew had stood in uncomfortable silence when Gar and Alea went apart—once they finally stopped staring at one another. Then they began to shift from foot to foot, studying the grass, the leaves, the trunks of the trees, and snatching furtive glances at one another. Finally, the third time she caught Kerlew looking at her, Moira laughed. "How silly we are! Can neither of us think of anything to say to the other?"

Her laugh sounded to Kerlew like the chiming of silver bells. He grinned shamefacedly and said, "I'm only a rough outlaw, a man cast out from his clan. What could I say to a fine lady?"

"Fine lady?" Moira smiled. "The only reason my clan didn't cast me out was because my parents did it for them, before I was born. Even the Druids wouldn't take me because I was too zealous about preaching for peace."

Kerlew lost his smile, but his eyes glowed. "That took a great deal of courage."

Moira smiled. "None dared touch me; I'm a seer, and they thought I was mad."

"Aye, for pleading the cause of peace," Kerlew said with disgust. "If that's madness, I hope it's catching."

"They seemed to feel it might be so." Moira's smile broadened; she felt a glow within. "Tell me, why were you outlawed?"

It seemed a rude question, but Kerlew told her quite frankly, "They thought me strange, probably rightly, and made fun of me for it. I tried to behave as they did, but the harder I tried, the more they mocked me—so I finally gave it up for a bad job and started telling them what I really thought of the feud."

"What is that?" Moira asked, her voice low.

"Why, that it's stupid and corrupted as a week-old carcass,"

Kerlew said, with feeling, "that it's cruel and vicious as an adder with its tail in a vise."

Moira blinked, startled by his intensity. "How did they take it?"

Kerlew shrugged. "As you would expect. They cast me out, and frightened though I was of the forest with its wolves and outlaws, I took it as a relief to be away from their torments." He smiled with sudden brilliance. "But an outlaw band took me in, and though they gave me their share of japes, they were never as bad as my clan. More to the point, they listened when I spoke against the feuds—and agreed with me!"

"Agreed with you?" Moira asked, startled. "Perhaps I've been speaking to the wrong people!"

"Why?" Kerlew asked practically. "It's the clans that start feuds, not the outlaw bands—unless they become big enough and old enough to start calling themselves a clan in their own right." He scowled, remembering Regan and her band.

"Become a clan, and start a feud of their own?"

"Not the feud yet, not the band I met with Gar, but they've only just begun to think of themselves as a clan. They'll find enemies soon enough, I know."

"I've heard of such." Moira smiled, reaching out for his hand. "So we're both outcast by our own choice, more or less, and both ready to plead the cause of peace."

Kerlew looked up in surprise. "Why yes, I suppose we are." Tentatively, he reached out and touched her fingers. There he froze, staring into her eyes, and might have taken firmer hold of her hand if Gar and Alea hadn't come back, glowing with enthusiasm and brimming with ideas.

The sentries of the Leary clan both raised their heads at the same moment. Samuel frowned. "Do you hear singing, Eliza?"

"Singing it is, and very pleasing too," Eliza answered. "Someone on the road knows harmony."

"Yeah, but who's creeping along with 'em in the brush?" Sam raised his rifle and shot into the air, high over the trees. "That oughta bring help if we need it."

"Didn't faze them any." Eliza looked down the road where the singing was growing louder.

"Wouldn't, if they know we're here and mean for their singing to draw our fire." Sam set his rifle stock on the ground, pulled the ramrod, and started reloading.

"Birds are still singing," Eliza noted. "They'd shut up if there were Clancies sneaking up in the brush."

"True enough." Sam raised his rifle again, frowning. "Might be just the three of them after all—no, four! There's a deeper voice under the three."

"Four there are." Eliza nodded. "And here they come!"

They came in sight, four walking side by side, filling the width of the road, the taller man and woman wearing the gray jackets of Druids, the younger man the blue of a bard, and the younger woman the green of a seer.

"Clerics!" Sam wrinkled his nose. "Might've known who'd be making such a racket."

The four came to a stop ten feet from the sentries, all smiling and cheery. "Hail, clansfolk!" the tall woman said. "We bear a message for you."

"A message?" Eliza asked warily. "For who?"

"For your whole clan!"

"Who from?" Sam asked, voice dripping skepticism.

"From the gods."

The sentries stared a moment. Then Sam turned away, fighting down laughter. Eliza managed to keep hers throttled down to a smile. "You still believe . . . No, of course you still believe in the gods—you're Druids."

Sam nodded, turning back with his laughter under control. "This is a bit big for us, Eliza. How about you take 'em back to the homestead?"

"And leave you here alone?" Eliza asked. "Not a bit! We'll wait for help."

"Help here," said a gruff voice. "What moves?"

Half a dozen clansfolk came down the path, rifles at the ready.

"Guests for the whole clan," Eliza told them. "Best take 'em to Grandma—they've got a message from the gods."

A couple of the younger people turned away to hide laughter. The older ones managed to confine their amusement to pinched smiles.

"Message from the gods, is it?" asked a woman whose coppery hair was streaked with white. "What do the gods want to tell us about, strangers?"

"Their displeasure," the tall man said, "and the punishment your clan has earned."

The throttled laughter died, the smiles ceased. The clanfolk stared at the strangers, and their stares weren't entirely friendly.

"The gods angry with us?" Grandma asked from her great chair by the fireplace. "What did you bring them in for, Eben? I've no need to hear nonsense like that!"

"I know, Ma," said a man with salt-and-pepper hair, "but we're obliged to be hospitable to strangers."

"Only if they mean us no harm!" Grandma scowled at the wanderers. Her hair was completely white, her face a network of wrinkles. Her wasted frame might have been robust and voluptuous in its day but was more bone than meat now. Nonetheless, her eye still gleamed with intelligence and her jaw was still firm with self-assurance. "If you come to curse us, strangers, you can keep right on going!"

"No harm intended," Gar answered, "unless you mean hurt to us or defiance to the gods."

Alea gazed off into space, raising her hands as she took on the appearance of a trance—and was surprised to feel some trace of rapport within her, some feeling of connection to a force greater than herself.

"What is this mummery?" one of the young men sneered.

"Be still, Rhys!" Grandma hissed. "She's making magic. Let's see if there's any worth to it."

Rhys glanced at the old woman as if wondering about her sanity, then back at Alea with the first hint of awe.

"I speak for Danu in her aspect as Mother of All People!" Alea said, not noticing that her voice had dropped several notes and gained resonance. "She who gives life to all is displeased with those who take it. She from whom the red blood springs is angered with those who squander the precious life force and spill the priceless current of their veins!" Then she staggered as though missing a step, eyes wide in surprise.

Gar glanced at her in concern.

Moira spoke up quickly. "I speak the words of Cathubovda!"

The clansfolk gasped, for Cathubovda was goddess of death and battle. You didn't have to believe in her to be upset at the mention of her name.

"We have served Cathubovda as well as though she were real." Grandma frowned. "We have been valiant in war, slain every enemy we could find, and cast out cowards and peacemongers from our ranks! What cause could Cathubovda have to be displeased with us?"

Moira stood, eyes upraised and unfocused, arms angled outward and downward, trembling. "Even Cathubovda wearies of excess! Slay strangers who come to you with fire and lead, not your own kind!"

"We do not!" Grandma Leary cried. "We slay only Clancies!"

"Celt must not kill Celt," Moira moaned. "Gaul must not slay Gael. The People of Danu must not murder one another, or there will be none left to fight when the Sassenach comes upon you." She threw back her head and gave vent to a weird warbling scream, eyes closing. "Cathubovda does as Danu bids! Cease this slaying of Danu's children, or Cathubovda shall strengthen your enemies against you! They shall lay waste your crops, they shall burn down your houses, they shall scatter the ashes and let the forest come back so that none shall know this clan ever stood!"

Breath hissed in, all about the chamber; wide eyes reflected lamplight. Even Grandma looked unnerved, but Rhys's lip curled. "So speak the women. What say you, boy?"

Grandma rounded on him, face purpling, but before she could speak Kerlew stepped forward, singing a high open ca dence, mockery dancing in his eyes, a smile of sarcasm showing teeth that gleamed in the firelight. Gar glanced at the boy and felt his blood run cold, for he could see that, like Moira, Kerlew believed his own role too well; the weird was upon him.

"So says the youth," he chanted, "so says the minstrel who honors Aengus."

People muttered to one another and someone even moaned, for Aengus was the Harper of the Dana, the Lord of the Land of Youth, who had gained his throne by trickery.

"Aengus, for the love of a maiden, sought the Land of Youth, where all was peace and harmony," sang Kerlew. "In his honor, I shall punish all who hinder peace, I shall discipline all who hinder love, I shall lay a satire upon all who harken not to the wishes of Danu!"

"A satire?" Rhys made a burlesque of cowering. "Oh, no! Not jokes! Not verses! Oh, how shall I defend myself against them?"

"How shall you defend yourself against your grandmother!" Grandma turned on the boy. "Fools should be still when wise folk speak!"

But before Rhys could respond, Kerlew began to chant:

"Your insults fly around,
No feet to touch the ground.
So who will watch your mouth when I'm away?
Every one steps back
For each slander you've attacked
Till you've none will call you kin or brother!"

A moment of preternatural stillness held the room. Then, almost imperceptibly, those nearest Rhys shifted their weight in such a way as to pull away from him a few inches. Someone said loudly, "Ridiculous!"

"To think a verse could change the way we think!" a woman agreed.

"Though you know, Rhys has always been kind of nasty," a third said.

"He has that," another woman concurred. "Now that I mind me of it, he did say some nasty spiteful things about you last winter, sister."

Kerlew stared, stupefied.

"Oh, really! Well, you should hear what he said about you when you were out of the room!"

"Can't really trust a man what'll talk behind your back," an older man growled.

"What are you talking about?" Rhys cried, turning from side to side to look at them all.

"If you can't trust him behind your back with words, you sure can't trust him with a rifle," someone else opined.

"You're talking trash!" Rhys protested. "You know I'm loyal to the clan!"

"To the clan, aye," Grandma snapped, "but to anybody in it? That's another story, isn't it, boy?"

Rhys spun to level a trembling forefinger at Kerlew. "This is your doing, stranger!"

Kerlew snapped out of his stupor and gave the young man a wicked grin. "Yes it is, and I could sing worse. How about if I tell them a man with a tongue as barbed as yours could only have been sired by a snake? Or that your boots are really hiding cloven hooves?"

Rhys paled. "They'd never believe it!"

"Are you sure?" Kerlew asked, then called out,

"A stranger he will slander rude,
But to his kin, why, he's a prude,
Careful to say only good.
Cherish him as ever you would!"

Everyone froze in a strange, still moment again. Then they relaxed, and a man called out, "You tell 'em, Rhys!"

"Aye!" cried a woman who'd protested about him moments before. "There's our lad!"

"Glad to have him beside me in battle, every time!" averred

the man who hadn't been willing to trust Rhys behind his back.

"A fine upstanding Leary, and a credit to his clan," Grandma said, nodding.

Rhys stared, jaw dropping.

Kerlew wasn't much better.

Then the young clansman turned on the bard. "You did that! All of it!"

Kerlew managed the wicked grin again. "Now imagine what would happen if I told them to cast you out—or told them all they were breaking out with boils!"

"You wouldn't dare!" Grandma gasped, but her face paled.

"I'll do what the gods tell me," Kerlew said bravely, then turned and called out to the assembly,

> *"Remember now each word you've said,*
> *About your kinsman Rhys—and dread*
> *The words that I may utter for*
> *The gods whose warnings you ignore!"*

The people gave their heads a quick shake, then looked at one another, appalled.

"Did I really say a thing like that?"

"Rhys, I'm sorry!"

"I can't believe I'd be telling such lies!"

"Rhys, I can't imagine what got into my head!"

"I can!" Rhys pointed a trembling finger at Kerlew. "His words!"

Everyone stared, then muttered with superstitious dread and moved a little farther away from the strangers.

Grandma appealed to Gar. "Bid him stop, stranger!"

"Stop?" Gar protested. "I haven't even told him to start! It's the gods who command him, Grandmother, not me!"

"All right, plead with your patron for us," Grandma growled. "Which god do you serve, anyway?"

"I speak the words of Taranis the Thunderer," Gar answered, "God of the Wheel and of Change!" His voice rose, carrying to the whole clan. "Do not kill anyone of your own kind, says Taranis—and your own kind is any Celt, any of the New People of this world!" His voice sank to an ominous rumble. "And of course, I do not need to tell you what would happen if you were to slay or even hurt one of the Old Ones!"

"Why should we heed what you say?" a clansman demanded angrily. "The gods are only stories for small children—they aren't real! All that's real is food and houses and rifles and gunpowder and bullets!"

The crowd muttered in answer, trying to work up enough anger to counter their sudden superstitious fear.

"Are your clothes real?" Gar demanded. "Are they as real as the cloth from which they were cut? Of course, for both were made by people! But was the cloth as real as the person who made it?"

"Why . . . of course." But the clansman sounded uncertain; he looked to his kinfolk for support.

"I see what you're saying." An old woman frowned at Gar. "We may be real, but not as real as the gods who made us. Trouble is, stranger, they may not be real at all—only one more thing that people made up, like a song or a dance!"

"If you invented the gods, then they stand for you," Gar countered. "Who is the patron of your clan?"

"Why . . . Toutatis," Grandma said, frowning. "But he's just a figurehead, a . . ." She left the sentence hanging, not wanting to finish the last word.

"Symbol?" Gar finished for her. "Then if you don't honor him, you don't honor your own clan—and if you fail to honor your clan, you fail to honor yourself."

"You don't mean we each have to have a god of our very own?" Rhys said, lip curling.

"Don't you?" Gar challenged. "When you were small and hearing the tales of the gods, wasn't there something within you that seized upon one god, one single one out of many, and said, 'Yes, this is my favorite!'"

Everyone looked astonished, then glanced quickly at his or her neighbors to see if they had noticed.

"Well . . . sure," Rhys said. "Doesn't everybody?"

"Everybody does," Gar agreed, "or if you can't find one, you develop your own picture of the Godhead, the ultimate God, your own understanding—and it helps you discover what kind of person you are, which is a very large step towards discovering *who* you are. Which god did you choose, young man?"

"Mider," Rhys admitted reluctantly, "the God of Good Judgment, the God of Common Sense."

"No wonder you insist on hearing proofs of what we claim!" Gar smiled. "And haven't you lived your life ever since as that god would have?"

"I see what you're saying!" the old woman cried. "If we don't respect our gods, we don't respect ourselves."

"Yourselves, each and every one of you." Gar nodded. "Yourselves as a clan—and yourselves as Celts, as New People, as human beings! Whether you believe in your gods or not, you must respect them or begin to fall apart!"

"Fall apart . . ." a few voices repeated, and people looked at one another in astonishment.

"And you'd have us respect the gods by doing as you tell us?" Grandma studied Gar from under lowering brows. "What else would they have us do besides stop killing?"

"Don't steal, not just from one another, but from other clans!"

A roar of protest answered him. Gar waited it out, then raised his arms. "Stealing started more feuds than one! Especially don't steal anybody's wife or husband either, not even for a few hours! That's the kind of thing can make clansman kill clansman."

"You're telling us the things that can make a clan fall apart," Grandma growled. "That's only common sense."

"Then you agree with it?"

"Within the Leary clan, yes. Clancies are another matter."

"Are they?" Gar demanded, looking Grandma straight in the eye. "How much of what you think to be their wickedness is really simple slander?" Grandma started to protest, but Gar's voice rode over hers as he turned to the people again. "The gods hate lies like that! Don't slander one another—no insults, no lies, no foul words aimed at other people! It might not only start a feud between clans—it might start a feud within a clan!"

The people stared at the thought, then shuddered.

"Speak truth or don't speak at all!" Gar orated. "Say 'yes' when you mean 'yes' and 'no' when you mean 'no'—and if you can't make up your mind, say so!"

"Next you'll be telling us not even to think of doing any of those," Grandma said with contempt.

"Think about them? You can't help some of that! You can't keep from wanting someone else's rifle, if it seems to be better than yours—or other people's spouses, especially if they're really good-looking. But you *can* keep from really trying to get them, planning for it, scheming for it. Will you or won't you, that's the question. Wanting it you can't help—willing it, you can, and shouldn't!"

"Anything else?" Grandma grated. "How many other laws will the gods load upon us?"

"Only those, and they're a lot fewer than the backbreaking load of laws your ancestors had before things fell apart. Anything else people are doing wrong, you can figure out from those."

"And that's all Taranis asks of us?" a clansman asked, looking worried.

"I'll make it simpler," Gar called out. "Respect your kinfolk and respect other clans as though they were kin, because somewhere far enough back, they are!"

Uproar filled the room. Gar waited it out, waited for the question he knew was coming, and finally Rhys voiced it. "What if we don't, stranger?" His eyes were hot, his voice acidic. "What if we don't choose to stop the feuding? What are you going to do—lay a satire on all of us?"

Kerlew nodded slowly, eyes glittering with all the bitterness and hatred of the outcast.

"Worse than that," Gar said quickly. "How would we know you were doing it, after all?"

"That's so!" A smiled curved Rhy's lips. "You can't punish what you don't see!"

"But the Old Ones will see you!" Gar called out. "The Wee Folk honor the gods, even the gods of the New People—and there are many, many of them: an elf in every pasture, a fairy in every tree!"

The people turned to one another in furious muttered debate and fear shone in many eyes. The gods' existence they might question, but nobody doubted the presence of the Wee Folk—their presence, or their power.

"Disobey the gods at your peril!" Gar cried out. "March to war against the Clancies and the Wee Folk will strike you down!"

The crowd's debate died down to a fearful mutter; lamplight reflected the whites of their eyes.

"All well and good," Grandma said sourly, "but what if the Clancies march against us? We're not going to stand there and let them butcher us!"

Half the clansfolk called out their agreement.

"We'll take the word of the gods to the Clancies next," Gar assured her. "If they march against you, the Little People will mow *them* down!"

"I'll believe that when I see it," Grandma snorted, "but if you're going to talk to them, stranger, you'd better hurry. Night's fallen, and they could be sending out ambush parties this very minute!"

"Oh, we'll tell them, and quickly," Gar assured her. "Come, friends!" He whirled away toward the door.

Alea pivoted to follow him. Kerlew and Moira stared, caught flat-footed, then hurried to catch up.

Gar turned about in the doorway, raising an arm in warning. "You've heard the word of the gods, and if you disobey it, there will be nothing I can do to save you! Farewell—and whether you believe in them or not, honor your gods!" With that, he spun about, cloak swirling, and strode off into the night, his companions around him.

The door closed behind them, and the clansfolk stood staring, frozen by the enormity of having seen and heard the unthinkable.

Then Grandma thawed and turned to Rhys. "Hurry! Send the captains out to the north pasture! Patrick's squad to the east boundary, hiding in the scrub brush! Caitlin's squad to the west windbreak, in among the pines! The rest of you move from cover to cover! If the Clancies are coming, we'll outflank them, and if they aren't, we'll take them by surprise while they're still numb from listening to those preachers!"

"But—but Grandma," said one of the middle-aged men, "the Old Ones . . ."

"You really believe what those addlepates said?" Grandma scoffed. "Mooncalves, every one of 'em—crazy as loons and wall-eyed as pikes! Old Ones obeying the New People's gods indeed! When have you ever known the Wee Folk to strike at more than one person at a time? What are you all, a bunch of overgrown children, ready to believe whatever song you're sung?"

That stung; the people frowned, anger stirring, muttering darkly.

"Out upon 'em, then!" Grandma called. "The Clancies just might believe those preachers, like the half-wits they are, and if they do, we'll never have a better chance of catching them with their guards down! Get out there into those woods and move silent as moonlight! Surround their house, then bust in and clean them out! when you're done, burn the place down for good measure! Go on, now, GO!"

16

Alea led the way out of the Clancy clan's great house and gazed up at the stars, drawing her cloak about her and shivering. "Midnight, Gar."

Gar nodded. "A good time for bad things to happen."

"Bad things indeed," Moira said darkly.

"You can feel them, can't you?" Alea asked Gar. "The Learies, moving up through the pitch-dark woods to surround this house?"

"How do you know that?" Kerlew asked, eyes wide.

"How do you make your satires actually hurt?" Gar countered.

"You'd better start composing them," Alea said, "one for the Learies and one for the Clancies."

"This can't be!" Kerlew protested. "They believed us!"

"Grandma Clancy didn't," Alea told him.

Moira's lips thinned. "She will when the Old Ones have done with them."

"The Learies are still half a mile away," Gar said, "and Grandma Clancy is back inside that house whipping her people into a fighting rage at the thought that the Learies might be creeping up on them like treacherous snakes."

"She should know," Moira said sourly. "Make that one satire against any who fight in defiance of Danu's wishes, Kerlew. Both bands mean mayhem."

"They do indeed," Alea agreed, "and we don't want to get caught between them when the bullets start flying. Come on, friends! Away from this place!"

They struck out uphill. Half an hour later and well above the treetops, they looked down on the Clancy homestead, tranquil in the still night—but Alea could read the homicidal thoughts both inside it and out, and shuddered.

She wasn't the only one. On the hillside across from hers, a furry globe-shaped alien with tiny cat-ears grinned, showing very sharp teeth. "Strike at the first shot," she told the gauzy-winged creature that hovered before her face. "Don't worry, I'll lend your minds more than enough power to lay them low. Has each one of your people chosen a Clancy?"

"Yes, and each elf is pacing a Leary, ready to fire a bolt," the fairy answered. "Speak, Bighead, and we shall loose our wrath upon them!"

A burst of flame blossomed in the woods below.

"Loose!" Evanescent snapped.

The sound of the shot reached them as several more fire-flowers bloomed at the narrow windows of the great house.

"Now do as my New People have promised," the alien purred, and sat back to watch the shortest war humans ever waged.

Aran Leary cried out and dropped his rifle, clutching his head as he sank to his knees.

"What ails you, Aran?" Caitlin cried.

Aran screamed and rolled on the ground.

"Rhys, see where he's shot!" Caitlin snapped. "Aran, cease that weakling's wailing! You want every single Clancy to know where we are?" As Rhys dove to see to Aran, Caitlin turned back to business, raising her rifle and sighting.

Fire flared in her belly. She dropped her weapon, folding over the pain, trying to stifle a scream and failing.

On the other side of the house, Patrick hissed, "Fire!" and a dozen Learies leveled their weapons, not seeing the darts that flew at them out of the darkness.

"Ow!" One swatted at his neck.

"Blast!" another clapped a hand over her arm. "What the blazes . . ."

"Damn big mosquitoes here!" A third clamped his lips against the urge to cry out. Then they all went rigid.

"What ails you slackers?" Patrick hissed. "Fire!" Then pain bit the back of his neck; he slapped at it, then froze. He tottered and fell just as his squad did, then screamed in agony as fire seemed to course through his veins.

Inside the house, Zachariah Clancy wondered, "Why the hell don't they shoot again?"

"We saw their rifle flashes," Amanda told him. "We can fire there again."

"A Leary just might be stupid enough to hang around waiting for a second shot," Zachariah allowed. "Let 'em have it!" Then he looked up, staring in disbelief out the window.

"Zachariah!" Malcolm cried. "Look there—a fairy!" Then he clutched his head and roared with pain.

Zachariah didn't pay much attention. He was too busy rolling on the floor and bellowing with pain of his own.

Atop the northern hill, Kerlew stood with his arms upraised, chanting,

> *The clansfolk now are terrified,*
> *For gods' commands are verified.*
> *Their geas of peace and amity has levied quite a strain.*

> *How can their disobedience be*
> *A source of mortal agony?*
> *In mind and soul their pain returns,*
> *To plague them once again!"*

He stood a moment, frowning down at the valley uncertainly, then turned to Gar and Alea. "How was that?"

"Not exactly great literature," Gar judged, "but it seems to have been effective."

"Too effective." Alea's face was strained; drops of sweat appeared on her brow. "At least, with help from the Old Ones, it is. Give them relief, Kerlew. Let's see if they've learned their lesson yet."

"As you say." Kerlew spread his hands and began to intone a verse that would relieve the pain.

On the southern hill, Evanescent looked up, reading his thoughts, then told the waiting fairy, "Give the New People a chance to reform. Take away their pain and see if they behave."

"Even so." The fairy turned and sang to another, who darted away into the night.

Minutes later, the Clancies all relaxed with a massive gasp, then pulled themselves up, blinking and white-eyed. Looking out through the windows, they remembered where they'd last seen their enemies. One or two reached for their rifles, then hesitated.

On the ground and in the trees, elves loosed more darts, and the Learies relaxed with shudders that shook their whole bodies, then slowly pushed themselves up to their knees. They looked down at their rifles, looked up at the darkened windows of the Clancy house, looked again at the rifles—but only looked.

Inside the house, Zachariah hobbled up to Grandma. "I don't know how that bard did it, Grandma, but everyone who aimed a rifle seized up with pain like we've never felt."

"I know," the old woman replied, white-knuckled and gasping. She looked up at Zachariah, her eyes rolling. "I felt it, too."

• • •

"They haven't started shooting again," Moira said.

"No, they haven't," Alea agreed, "but that doesn't mean they won't, as soon as they think we've gone."

"Then we'd better stay," Gar said. "Kerlew, you'd better compose some new verses, just in case."

Both sides stayed in place, watching through the night, hands never far from their rifles but never quite touching, either. As the stars began to dim, Aran said to Amanda, "I've been thinking."

"What?" she asked, exhaustion making her voice ragged.

"It was the bard who laid the satire on us that's caused this pain, right?"

"I figured that out for myself," she said with withering sarcasm.

"Okay, how about this? We kill the bard and we kill the pain!"

Amanda was silent for several minutes, staring out the window at the dark masses of bushes that hid Learies. Finally she announced her verdict: "Won't work. It's the Old Ones who are bringing the pain, just as the satire told them. They'll still heed its words whether the bard's there or not."

Aran growled resentment. "Why should the Old Ones obey a bard all of a sudden?"

"Because this one's satires really work," Amanda answered. "Who knows what verses he laid on the Wee Folk?"

Aran was silent awhile, seething with frustration and anger. Finally he said, very softly, "How about if we kill the Old Ones?"

Pain ripped through his head. He clutched his hair, rolling on the floor, choking down screams into a gargling mutter. Then the pain ceased and he went limp, panting.

Amanda looked down on him with sympathetic eyes but said, "No. I don't think we'd better try that."

• • •

Outside, Patrick slipped through the gloaming to his fellow captain. "Caitlin," he said, "when did the Old Ones become this mighty?"

"Guess they always have been, Pat," she answered. "They just never thought to use the full weight of their power before."

Patrick frowned. "What made 'em do it now?"

"The bard," Caitlin answered.

"Yeah, the bard," Patrick growled in disgust, "and it's the priests and the seer who've made him realize he can do it."

Caitlin turned a cold glance on him. "What damnfool notion are you cooking up?"

"You know," he said.

"Then its damnfool indeed!" she answered. "Those fairies and elves know what they can do now! Killing the bard and the priests won't change that."

Patrick turned to gaze out at the dark bulk of the house, scowling. After a while, he said, "The seal's been broke and the jar's opened. No way to lock it tight again, is there?"

"Not unless you got one hell of a kettle to boil it in," Caitlin answered, "no."

Atop the northern hill, Kerlew asked anxiously, "Will they try to fight again?"

Gazing off into the darkness but seeing another world, Moira told him, "No. They're too smart for that."

Alea nodded. "They've thought it out and found it's too late to stop the Old Ones."

"You mean they're afraid of elves and fairies?"

"Not afraid," Gar said. "In fact, they could probably withstand the pain long enough to loose a few shots now and then— but only a few. They've begun to realize that the feuds are going to be too difficult to manage any more."

"You mean the price is too high?" Kerlew asked.

"The price has always been too high," Moira answered, tight-lipped.

Alea nodded. "But so far, they've had a chance of winning.

Now they know that they'll all lose, and nobody can win any battle."

"As they should have all along," Gar said.

"So they'll stop feuding because the cost is too high?" Kerlew asked. "Not because it's wrong?"

Alea gazed off into space, sampling the thoughts below her. Then she reported, "One or two of them are beginning to think that. Just one or two, mind you."

"But it's not even morning yet," Moira reminded her.

Inside the great house, Aran said slowly, "You don't suppose the gods are real, do you?"

A week later, neither Clancy nor Leary had moved to attack the other again, though each still kept its sentries stationed round the clock. Monitoring their thoughts, Alea found that each clan had told its neighbors about the episode. Two of those neighbors had marched out for a final battle before the Druids managed to reach them with their message of peace or doom, but as soon as any of them put finger to trigger, they collapsed in agony. There were many, many Old Ones, and they were watching all the New Folk like hawks.

So, when the sky lightened a fortnight after the abortive battle, Alea and Gar led Moira and Kerlew up to the bald top of a high hill, then turned to reassure them.

"They'll only need reminding from now on," Alea told the two young folk. "The rumor mill is in full swing, and half the land has already heard that the gods have finally forbidden the feuding."

"But what if they ambush us to keep us from preaching to them?" Kerlew asked, eyes wide with fright.

"How can we manage without you now?" Moira cried.

"Quite well, I think," Gar told them. "Wherever you go now, the Old Ones will be watching—and anyone who makes any move to hurt you will feel as though he's been plunged into fire."

"Or will wake up the day after you've passed and wonder what put him to sleep," Alea added. "If a whole clan chases you, you've only to run to the nearest fairy Mound, and the Keepers will give you sanctuary. No one will dare follow you onto the slopes of the Mound itself."

They could see the edge of hysteria fade from the eyes of the young folk, see them stand a little straighter, a little more firmly, even though Moira said, "What if they simply lurk in the woods around the Mound and wait for us to come out?"

"Then you have simply to wait until the Old Ones drive them away," Alea told her. "If they won't scare from simple accidents, a few heart attacks and even one or two dead will certainly make them go."

"Besides," Gar said, "even if some assassin does manage to get past your elfin bodyguards, do you really think this cause isn't worth your life?"

"Of course it is," Kerlew said instantly, his jaw squaring with obstinacy.

"My life, yes." Moira glanced at the young man out of the corner of her eyes. "His life, no."

"But your life is more important than mine!" He turned to take her hands. "I can't go on preaching and wandering without you! Besides, who'd listen to the bard without the seer?"

Moira stared into his eyes for a long moment, then said, "I guess we'll have to travel together, won't we?"

The morning seemed suddenly filled with amazing tension.

Kerlew's voice was low. "Be careful what you say. This is no summer's jaunt we're setting out on. There's no way out once we start it. If we're into this at all, we're into it for life."

"We're already into it." Moira clasped his hands with both of hers. "For all our lives."

"Together," he whispered.

They stood in silence, staring into one another's eyes.

"At least you gave me more of an option than that," Alea said to Gar with an impish smile.

Shutters seemed to come down behind his eyes; he nodded gravely. "Of course. Any planet you choose to stay on, you shall. I'd never try to haul you off against your will."

Alea stared up at him, appalled, and thought came in a rush of feeling, but she was careful to shield the words from his mind. *Blast! Now I've gone and hurt him again! A curse on she who shattered his fragile heart!*

Moira turned to them with a smile. "And if she chooses to stay with you?"

Gar stared at her, taken aback, then slowly smiled. "I'll rejoice in her company, of course."

Alea flashed the younger woman a grateful smile.

But Kerlew frowned. "What's a planet?"

"A wandering star," Gar answered, "a world, like this one."

Moira stared, then darted a glance at the paling vault above them, the scattering of stars still visible. "Each one of them a world?"

"Most of them are suns," Gar corrected, "but there are many, many planets, as well."

Kerlew stared upward, too. "You don't mean you travel from planet to planet!"

"We do," Alea said with a gentle smile.

"But how?"

"In a ship that sails between the stars." Gar pointed at the sky. "That one."

Moira and Kerlew stared up in disbelief as the great golden disk spun lower and lower.

In a grove at the edge of the hilltop, an elf protested, "But we won't have strength enough to stop the feuds without you!"

"You won't," Evanescent acknowledged, "but the New People won't know that. Just pick out the odd rifle-bearer now and then, gang up on him, and send him into half a minute of agony. The tale will run and the New People will obey the laws of bard and seer, for fear of you."

"And of their gods," sang a fairy by the alien's brow.

Evanescent nodded. "After a while, they'll even begin to believe in their gods again, yes."

"Still, you can't leave us," the elf pointed out. "How will you climb aboard that ship without their knowing?"

"Why, like this." Evanescent watched Gar and Alea stop at the top of the boarding ramp to wave at Kerlew and Moira, then turn to go into the ship. The younger couple turned to talk to one another in stunned amazement as the ramp started to lift. Then, suddenly, they froze, and so did the ramp.

"You can control their minds that well!" the fairy marvelled.

"And their ship's," Evanescent said, "though it hasn't a mind, really, only a machine that imitates one."

"But it will remember."

"No, I'll erase all memory of me from the ship's data banks," Evanescent explained. "From the minds of the bard and seer, too. That's a trick you might want to learn; it can come in handy from time to time."

The fairy exchanged a surprised glance with the elf. "Yes, I can see that it would."

"Good luck to you, then." Evanescent shouldered out of the shrubbery. "Now I must go. I really shouldn't keep them waiting."

"May you fare well," the fairy told her, and the elf agreed, "May your journey be light."

Or light-years, Evanescent thought smugly. Then she waddled over to the ramp, leaped up onto it, and scuttled aboard. Seconds later, the ramp slid back into the ship and Moira looked up. Kerlew followed her gaze, and the two of them stood watching as the golden disk rose slowly, then suddenly streaked back into the sky, alight with the sunrise.

Aboard the ship, Alea came into the lounge in her robe, a towel wound turbanlike around her hair, to find a tall iced drink waiting next to her lounger. She slid into it, took a long sip, then looked up at Gar, secure and amazingly relaxed in a velvet robe, one hand on his iced glass, head leaning back against the padding, eyes closed.

"Where to next, O Mighty Hunter?" Alea asked.

"Why, where you will," Gar replied, not opening his eyes.

Alea stared. "You expect me to choose the next planet? All on my own?"

"If you want to." Gar's eyelids cracked open to gaze at her, a peaceful smile on his lips. "If you don't, give me a week or two to rest and look through the database."

"Well . . . I could use a rest, too." Alea eyed him with concern. "Somehow I thought you already had the look of a man on the brink of his next journey, though."

"Perhaps I am." Gar closed his eyes, and the image of the rag-and-bone man rose unbidden behind his eyelids. "There is an unknown land I need to explore. I've been putting it off a while."

Alea tried to keep the concern out of her voice. "You'll need a companion, then."

"Perhaps I will." Gar opened his eyes again just enough to give her a lazy, trusting smile. "But I can wait. There will be time."

"There will be time," Alea echoed him in a whisper and, since his eyes were closed, let herself simply sit and gaze at his rough-hewn features in a very rare moment of tranquility.

In the ship's hold, in an area where Herkimer's sensors had strangely ceased to send signals to the computer's CPU (and, more strangely, Herkimer wasn't aware of the fact), Evanescent the alien settled down to hibernate, gleefully remembering that Alea hadn't realized the extent of the alien's meddling. None of them had so much as guessed that it was she who sent the disorientation that had broken up the battle between the Belinkuns and the Farlands, she who had sent Kerlew a vision of a sick woman miles away, she who had helped Gar confuse the members of the large outlaw band who chased him and Kerlew, she who had made Kerlew's satire of the clan leader produce pain, she who had helped the fairies and Wee Folk stop this last battle. Her absence wouldn't matter, though—she had already told the Old Ones how to cope without her, and Kerlew's latent psi talent had burgeoned with her help. His satires would be quite effective with no power but his own now.

Of course, Alea couldn't have guessed at the alien's efforts, since Evanescent never let her remember their encounters. She toyed with letting the young woman recover those memories for a little while aboard ship, then rejected the plan. Time enough to let Alea remember when Evanescent needed another conference with her.

All in all, the alien reflected, it had been a most enjoyable interlude, a delightful relief from boredom, but tiring, too. She was looking forward to a nice long nap. Lazily, she directed one last thought at Gar and Alea, making them want rest as much as she did, then let herself sink down through layers of dwindling consciousness to the land of very exotic dreams that no human being could possibly have understood.